The Doctor's Secret Son

Deb Kastner

Love Inspired

LOVE INSPIRED BOOKS

Recycling programs for this product may not exist in your area.

ISBN-13: 978-0-373-87718-8

THE DOCTOR'S SECRET SON

www.LoveInspiredBooks.com

Printed in U.S.A.

Hadn't anything else scandalous happened in the ten years she'd been gone?

It seemed to her everyone had far too keen of memories where she and Zach were concerned.

Delia had a hard time breaking her gaze away from Zach. He took one step toward her and then stopped, undecided.

Alexis, Mary and Samantha stood and hovered around Delia until she, too, came to her feet.

But instead of meeting her halfway, Zach stepped sideways and planted his hat on his head.

"Ladies," he murmured with a clipped nod. A moment later he was striding out the door and down the road.

Delia was equally distressed and relieved. She didn't care for him brushing her off with such callousness, but she wasn't quite ready to talk to him, either. She didn't yet know how to say what needed to be said, nor when would be the best time to do it.

Maybe there was no best way to say it.

Zach, you have a son.

Books by Deb Kastner

Love Inspired

A Holiday Prayer
Daddy's Home
Black Hills Bride
The Forgiving Heart
A Daddy at Heart
A Perfect Match
The Christmas Groom
Hart's Harbor
Undercover Blessings
The Heart of a Man
A Wedding in Wyoming
His Texas Bride
The Marine's Baby
A Colorado Match
*Phoebe's Groom
*The Doctor's Secret Son

*Email Order Brides

DEB KASTNER

lives and writes in colorful Colorado with the Front Range of the Rocky Mountains for inspiration. She loves writing for Love Inspired Books, where she can write about her two favorite things—faith and love. Her characters range from upbeat and humorous to (her favorite) dark and broody heroes. Her plots fall anywhere in between, from a playful romp to the deeply emotional. Deb's books have been twice nominated for the *RT Book Reviews* Reviewers' Choice Award for Best Book of the Year for Love Inspired. Deb and her husband share their home with their two youngest daughters. Deb is thrilled about the newest member of the family—her first granddaughter, Isabella. What fun to be a granny! Deb loves to hear from her readers. You can contact her by email at Debwrtr@aol.com, or on her MySpace or Facebook pages.

Dear Reader,

Welcome to Love Inspired!

2012 is a very special year for us. It marks the fifteenth anniversary of Love Inspired. Hard to believe that fifteen years ago, we first began publishing our warm and wonderful inspirational romances.

Back in 1997, we offered readers three books a month. Since then we've expanded quite a bit! In addition to the heartwarming contemporary romances of Love Inspired, we have the exciting romantic suspenses of Love Inspired Suspense, and the adventurous historical romances of Love Inspired Historical. Whatever your reading preference, we've got fourteen books a month for you to choose from now!

Throughout the year we'll be celebrating in several different ways. Look for books by bestselling authors who've been writing for us since the beginning, stories by brand-new authors you won't want to miss, special miniseries in all three lines, reissues of top authors and much, much more.

This is our way of thanking you for reading Love Inspired books. We know our uplifting stories of hope, faith and love touch your hearts as much as they touch ours.

Join us in celebrating fifteen amazing years of inspirational romance!

Blessings,

Melissa Endlich and Tina James
Senior Editors of Love Inspired Books

To my grandchildren, Isabella and Anthony.
You are the future of our family's faith.

* * *

Therefore, as the elect of God, holy and beloved,
put on tender mercies, kindness, humbleness of
mind, meekness, longsuffering; Bearing with one
another and forgiving one another; Even as
Christ forgave you, so you also must do.
But above all these things put on love,
which is the bond of perfection.
—*Colossians* 3:12–14

Prologue

Text Message

Riley Ivers: My mom is crying. She just got off the phone with Grandpa.

Justin Sanderson: What's up?

Riley Ivers: She says we have to move.

Justin Sanderson: Dude, tell her the house next door to mine has a For Sale sign out front.

Riley Ivers: I wish. My grandma's sick. We have to move near her.

Justin Sanderson: Where?

Riley Ivers: Texas.

Justin Sanderson: No way!

Riley Ivers: I don't want to move away from Baltimore.

Justin Sanderson: Tell her you don't want to go.

Riley Ivers: I did. She said she doesn't want to go, either, but we have to 'cause of Grandma.

Justin Sanderson: Oh, man.

Riley Ivers: This stinks.

Chapter One

Medical emergencies were few and far between in Serendipity, Texas. Delia Rae Ivers wasn't sure she'd ever readjust to the sleepy pace of the town where she'd been born. She hadn't so much as visited for years, and now suddenly she was living and working here. After a busy emergency room setting at the Baltimore hospital she'd interned at, being a small-town doctor was going to take some getting used to.

She leaned back in the leather chair behind her desk and stretched wearily. She was a doctor, not an accountant, and squinting at numbers for hours as she examined the small medical clinic's financials and then entered them into her computer was not her idea of fun.

"Riley, buddy, are you finished counting the gauze rolls?" she called to her son. They'd arrived in town only five days ago, and Riley hadn't yet met any kids his age, so Delia had given him small tasks to do around the clinic to keep him busy and out from underneath his grandparents' feet.

"I'm done, Mom." Riley peeked his head around the corner of the back office door and a lock of shaggy black hair flopped over his forehead. No matter how he tried to comb it, his thatch of hair stubbornly spiked hopelessly in every direction.

"And the boxes of gloves? Did you get those, too?"

"Yeah, I did."

Delia's gaze dropped to the toy car her son was clasping in his left hand. Clearly he was getting bored counting medical inventory, and she couldn't blame him. It wasn't exactly the most exciting job in the world, especially for a nine-year-old boy. Gentle waves of love lapped in her heart. Riley was her world, and had been from the moment he was born.

"I have another project for you," she informed him, pinching back the smile that would give her away.

Riley groaned. "Oh, Mom."

"I think you'll like this." She let her smile emerge. "You know that little alcove—room—in the back corner of the waiting room? The one that's set up for kids to play in?"

Riley nodded. His eyes glinted with interest, but she could tell his concentration was still focused on the car in his hand.

"I bought a video game system and a small television to hook up in there so the older kids have something to do while they wait."

"Way cool!"

She chuckled. Now she *knew* she had her son's full attention.

"I need to get it hooked up. Think you can do that for me?"

At age nine, Riley was heads-and-tails above Delia in the electronics department. When it came to video games and televisions, and even computers, he already knew more than she ever would. She had no doubt that he'd have the system up and running in no time. As she'd said, it *was* for the kids; but most especially, it was for Riley. She knew there'd be times he would be stuck at the clinic waiting for his mom to finish work. Now he'd have something to keep him occupied.

"The TV and the video system are already in the room, so whenever you're ready..." Her sentence drifted to a halt as Riley sprinted from the room. Delia smiled.

Poor Riley hadn't wanted to move, especially two weeks before Christmas and Delia couldn't say that she blamed him. This wouldn't have been her first choice, either—or *any* choice, for that matter. But her mother, with her worsening multiple sclerosis, needed the kind of care only a nursing facility could give her—or a live-in doctor.

Delia had the right training. Could she do any less for the family she loved?

She'd soon discovered she was needed in other ways, too. Her email had been overflowing since she'd announced her return. Friends were quick to remind her that old Doc Severns had retired a few months back, and the entire town was without a practicing M.D. Serendipity's clinic had been closed. Now that Delia had moved back, she intended to take over the practice. Not only would she be able to help her own mother, but she could also make a real difference in the community—to the friends and neighbors she'd grown up with and still cared about.

She sighed and brushed her long, straight black hair back with her fingers. Even with all of the dynamic changes in her life, it wasn't so much the future that weighed so heavily on her mind.

It was the past.

Zach Bowden, to be precise.

Serendipity's own James Dean in faded jeans and a white T-shirt, with dreamy poet eyes and bad boy ways. Trouble with a capital *T.* The man she'd left behind but had never forgotten. The only man who'd ever completely captured her heart.

And her worst nightmare.

Zach was the reason Delia had left town so suddenly all those years ago, and he was the reason she'd never returned to Serendipity, not even to visit. Even with all the time that had passed, *he* was the reason she was having such a hard time concentrating on the books. She couldn't get him out of her mind.

Serendipity was a very small town. Sooner or later the two of them would cross paths, and when they did, Delia had no doubt that her life would go into a tailspin.

So, for that matter, would Zach's, when he found out the truth about why she'd stayed away.

And Riley?

Her decision to move home had everything to do with her son, who had recently started asking tough questions about his father, painful questions Delia had been unable to answer. It was her deepest fear that Riley would be the one most injured by the choices she'd made—and was making now.

A persistent knot throbbed behind her left eye. She rubbed her temple to relieve the pounding pain. Between accounting and Zach, it would be almost impossible for her to avoid a headache, both literally and figuratively.

No matter how she felt, she had to press on. The only way to look to the future here in Serendipity was to settle the past. Do the right thing—whatever that was. For Delia, the lines between right and wrong had been cloudy and gray for years.

She tried to turn her mind back to the present, but she found it difficult to concentrate. Math had never been her strong suit. She retrieved the pencil she'd tucked behind her ear and wiggled the computer mouse so the screen would come back to life. The software she was using was supposed to help, but instead it managed to confuse her all the more.

She could do this, she reminded herself.

Financials were part and parcel of operating a small-town clinic. For now, she needed to conquer the numbers on her own. Although, later, she planned to hire a receptionist to take up much of the slack.

A steady, persistent knock startled Delia and she jerked up in surprise. No one should be here yet. The sign in the window still said that the clinic was closed for business, and she wasn't expecting any deliveries this afternoon; but whoever was rapping on the rear door was certainly insistent.

Still a little hazy from the mental strain of bookkeeping and the emotional strain of moving home to Serendipity, she went to see who it was. An ambulance had backed up within feet of the clinic doors, the lights still flashing. She realized that she must have been completely lost in her thoughts, for she hadn't heard a siren, although she supposed it was possible they hadn't used one.

Nonetheless, her mind instantly shifted into doctor mode. Adrenaline pumped through her and erased all the fogginess from her brain. She didn't give a thought to the fact that she was not officially open for business. Someone needed help. That's what she was here for.

Her focus was completely on the patient as the EMT who'd been driving moved around to the back of the ambulance and swung the doors open. She recognized the first paramedic, Ben Atwood, and she knew the man strapped to the gurney—Drew "Spence" Spencer, the fifth-grade teacher at the elementary school in town. He was attached to an IV and his face was bunched up in pain as he cradled his left arm to his chest.

She held open the door and gestured them inside as the second EMT exited the ambulance and moved to the other side of the gurney to help guide it in.

"You know Drew Spencer."

Delia's breath caught as she flashed her gaze to the paramedic who was speaking to her.

Zach.

Her heart slammed to a halt and then lurched back into action. Zach's voice had deepened some, but even after all these years, she recognized his distinctive honey-rich drawl immediately.

How could it be that Zach was an emergency medical technician? Not only that, but an unpaid *volunteer,* as the tri-county fire department couldn't afford a full-time staff.

She was so surprised that a proverbial feather could have knocked her over. Zach had never cared for anyone but himself—he'd proven that more times than she cared to count.

She felt as if she were participating in a strobe-lit, slow-motion theater scene as she turned to lock eyes with her old flame. Surely the distance, the time, would make some sort of difference in her feelings for him, or at least mute them in some way.

Back then she'd been young. Irrational. Naive.

And totally in love.

She knew better now.

But the moment her gaze met the dreamy chocolate depths of his eyes, she realized nothing had changed. It was as if the years between them hadn't passed at all, if her heart had anything to say about it.

One corner of his lips twitched upward in a lady-killer smile that had sent more than one young woman's heart aflutter. He took a deep breath and exhaled and Delia realized she was breathing right in synch with him.

He was still incredibly good-looking in that rough-edged, bad boy way of his. Her gaze slid over him, remembering every detail of his lean, muscular six-foot frame.

His wind ruffled, shaggy brown hair was cut only marginally shorter than it had been when he was younger. The straight nose and strong jaw were the same—although his skin was more weathered and there were stress lines on his face. A haunted, pained expression had replaced the jaunty, carefree attitude he'd carried as a youth.

Without giving it a second thought, she took a couple of steps toward him.

"Zach," she murmured.

He reacted as if she'd pushed him, jerking his shoulder away and stepping hastily backward out of her reach. A muscle twitched in the corner of his jaw as he broke his gaze away from her.

She experienced a stab of something suspiciously

like rejection, but that only lasted for a second before panic set in.

Zach was here. And Riley was in the next room.

Her heart beat frantically as she considered her options, not that she had any. She could hardly bolt out of the room to go get Riley and then run away and hope Zach didn't see them.

She didn't know when—or even if—she was going to tell Zach he had a son; but definitely not this soon. Not in these circumstances. She could only hope Riley was too caught up in setting up the video system to bother checking out what was happening in the exam room.

Mindfully, and with all the willpower she possessed, she calmed her nerves and turned her attention to her patient, where it belonged.

Zach's introduction of Spence had been a little off-script for what one would expect in a big hospital. But this was Serendipity, which was an extremely close-knit community. Everyone literally *did* know everyone. She'd gone to school with Spence, although he'd been several grades above her.

"He has second-degree burns on his left hand and forearm," Zach continued crisply as he hung the IV bag on a hook on the wall and then helped his partner transfer Spence to the examining table. "His vitals are stable and we gave him morphine for the pain. Under normal circumstances we would have taken him to the nearest hospital, but I thought we should get his wound looked at as soon as possible, and now that you're here in town…well, I hope you don't mind that we brought him here to the clinic."

"No, no, I don't mind at all. I'm happy you thought

of me." Actually, she had all kinds of conflicting emotions about the idea that Zach had *thought* of her, but again she willfully tucked her feelings into the back of her heart to scrutinize later.

"My father went and called 9-1-1 after I asked him not to," Spence explained in a raspy tone. "I really didn't need an ambulance."

"Sure you did," Ben disagreed affably. He and Zach supported Spence as he transferred himself from the gurney to the examining table.

"You're just too stubborn to admit it," Zach added with a chuckle.

Even though Delia didn't say so aloud, she agreed with Zach and Ben. She was glad old Frank Spencer had responded with an emergency call. Spence might not have thought he needed attention, but burns were nothing to play with.

"You've got this?" Ben asked Zach.

Zach's lips flattened into a straight line, but after a moment he gave Ben a clipped nod.

Ben looked from Zach to Delia and back, his expression unconvinced. Everyone in this town knew Zach and Delia's history together. Ben was no doubt wondering if leaving them alone together was the best idea.

"We're fine," Delia assured him.

Ben tapped his clipboard and nodded, and then turned for the door. "I'll get to the paperwork, then."

"So what have we got here?" she asked her patient. Wrapping a blood pressure cuff around Spence's right arm, she leaned over the grimacing man and carefully drew back the blanket that covered his left hand.

The area across the back of his hand and halfway up his forearm was red and blistered, but Delia was relieved to find it looked no more serious than a second-degree burn, something she could treat here at the clinic.

Spence grimaced and Zach moved to his side, laying his large, reassuring hand on Spence's shoulder.

"Hang in there, buddy," he murmured gently.

Delia felt a wave of emotion reach her throat at the kindness in his words and actions. She was completely unprepared for the sizzling epiphany that reached both her heart and her head at the same time.

Zach wasn't the boy she had left behind.

He was a man now, and not just in the way his lanky teenaged frame had filled out with solid muscle, either. For whatever reason, he volunteered his time and capability in a career dedicated to helping others. It wasn't his usual self-centered M.O., or at least it hadn't been, and she realized it would take her awhile to change her perspective. She'd grown up—she was far different from the teenager she'd been when she left.

Perhaps Zach was different, too—maturing into the man standing with her now.

She hoped her observations about Zach had at least some basis in truth. Riley needed a good, stable influence from his father, not the hot-cold, on-again/off-again relationship she feared might happen.

Had Zach changed—or was it just that paramedic work provided the adrenaline that he so craved? It was still too soon to tell.

"How did this happen, Spence?" she queried gently as she unwrapped the wound.

"I was boiling water," Spence explained, wincing. "The twins' favorite meal is spaghetti."

Delia smiled and arched her brows as she closely examined the red and blistering skin. Keeping a patient talking kept his mind off the pain. "I didn't know you had children. Boys? Girls?"

"Boys. Matty and Jamey. They just turned three and they're a real handful, let me tell you."

Delia thought of Riley at age three and had to agree, if only to herself. Obviously she couldn't say what she was thinking out loud.

"Really cute little buggers," Zach confirmed with a grin, though he didn't look at Delia when he spoke. "They're both on the junior T-ball team I coach every spring. They'll be ready to move up into the major leagues pretty soon."

Zach was a *coach?*

For a kid's team?

She was equally relieved and flustered by the new information, but she'd learned a long time ago the necessity of compartmentalizing her thoughts and feelings when she was dealing with a patient. Right now her mind had to be on her work.

"So your burn is from the water?" she asked, turning Spence's hand over to examine the palm.

"Yeah, that and the steaming pot. One of the twins screamed and I lost my focus—just for a moment. When I turned back to the stove, the water was overflowing. I scrambled to take the pot off the burner barehanded, without even thinking about what I was doing."

"Looks like you scalded yourself pretty good, buddy," Zach said in a gentle, teasing voice.

Spence grimaced. "Pretty stupid, huh?"

"No, of course not," Delia replied. "Accidents happen. Don't worry. I can fix you up."

Just for a moment, her gaze met Zach's. His eyes were surprisingly full of compassion.

"Happens to the best of us, big guy." Zach winked at his neighbor. "I've had my fair share of accidents myself."

That was an understatement if Delia had ever heard one.

Zach Bowden was an accident waiting to happen, and Delia wasn't positive she was any more prepared for him this time around than she had been as a teenager.

She continued to examine Spence without blinking an eye, but internally she was in turmoil. She might be able to fool the others but she could never fool herself. Today's encounter with Zach had changed the playing field entirely, and she didn't know what to do with what she had learned.

She didn't know the man Zach Bowden had become.

Worse yet, she wasn't over him.

Chapter Two

On the outside, at least, Zach kept his attention on his ailing neighbor, but, surreptitiously, he watched Delia work, his heart drinking in the presence of the woman who had once been his whole life like a man who'd spent years in the desert with no water.

In a way, that was exactly what he was. He had told himself a million times that he wouldn't care if he ever saw Delia again in his life, but he now knew that was a flat-out lie.

How could he *not* care when she had taken his heart and smashed it into thousands of pieces?

Time hadn't healed his wounds, nor had it changed the way his heart leaped out of his chest every time their eyes met. It shook him to the core to discover that despite the anger and bitterness he felt toward her, his attraction to her had only deepened with the passage of time.

She was beautiful.

She'd always been pretty, but now there was a new maturity shining from those huge sapphire-blue eyes of hers. Her black hair, which she'd worn shoulder-length as a teen, now flowed in thick, glossy waves down her back. Her rich alto voice had matured to be smooth as silk, wrapping around a man's senses like a warm wind.

"On a scale of one to ten, with ten being the worst pain you can imagine, how do you feel?" Delia asked Spence in a soft, reassuring tone.

"Still about a five or six," Spence said with a groan. "Man, this really hurts."

"That's actually good news," Delia informed him, and Zach silently concurred. "When you really start to worry about a burn is if it doesn't hurt at all."

"Great," Spence muttered.

Delia chuckled.

Zach squeezed the man's shoulder as Delia added additional morphine to the IV and efficiently prepared a cart for dressing the wound.

"It looks worse than it is," he assured Spence. "Right, Delia?"

"Absolutely. You'll need to change the dressing a couple of times a day and take the antibiotics I'm going to prescribe you, but this should heal up just fine. I'll clean up the wound a bit and you'll be as good as new."

Spence's gaze widened perceptibly, but he clenched his jaw and nodded gravely as he resolved himself to endure the discomfort.

Zach felt for him. Burns really hurt, even the small ones, and even though Spence's burn wasn't life-threatening, he'd still have to struggle with the pain.

"Do you feel the narcotic kicking in yet?" Zach asked as the tension left Spence's shoulders.

Spence's eyes grew dilated and hazy, and he laid his head back on the pillow and sighed. "Yes, thankfully."

"Just keep your eyes on me, man," Zach suggested.

"This will all be over in a minute. You can trust Delia. She's a great doctor."

Delia's surprised gaze flew to Zach, and it was no wonder. In truth, he had no way of knowing what kind of a doctor Delia was. He'd made the comment for Spence's benefit, to ease his anxiety.

That said, he was fairly certain his statement was correct. Even though he'd never actually seen Delia practice medicine, he had no doubt in his mind that she was a very good doctor. As long as he'd known her, she'd dreamed of having a career in the medical field. She'd always excelled as a student. And she was nothing if not persistent and dedicated. She wouldn't let any obstacle get in the way of whatever she wanted to do.

Even if *he* was the obstacle in question.

He ignored the tug in his gut and reminded himself to keep his mind on his work. This was no time to visit the past.

Delia was quick and efficient as she cleaned and dressed the wound. Zach imagined she'd encountered dozens of similar situations on her emergency room rotations in Baltimore, although this time her patient was a neighbor, a man she'd known from her childhood.

How did she feel about being able to provide medical assistance to someone she was acquainted with? Did she find the same satisfaction in helping a friend as he did?

Maybe that's why she'd finally come home.

He experienced another acute, agonizing stab in his gut. Unlike Spence's burn, which probably would do little more than leave a scar, Zach's wounds had never quite healed properly, and he didn't think they ever would.

Delia reached for a key to the medicine cabinet and provided Spence with a bottle of prescription painkillers and an antibiotic. She was the pharmacist as well as the doctor in this little town; but, as with the rest of her duties, she handled the transaction with ease.

She rechecked the wound one last time and pronounced Spence good to go.

"Ben and I can give you a lift back to your house," Zach suggested, supporting Spence's arm as he rolled to a sitting position.

"I've already caused you enough grief," Spence argued. "I can find some other way home."

Delia's gaze shifted to Zach. She knew him well enough to know he wasn't going to back down. That wasn't his way.

"Nonsense," Zach said with a shake of his head. "It makes sense for us to give you a ride. Your father can't drive anymore, and even if he could, he's the one who's watching the twins."

"Yes, but—"

Zach cut him off with a wave of his hand. "Ben and I will be happy to take you. Not another word, you understand?"

Even after Zach's friendly warning, Spence still looked like he was about to argue some more, at least until Delia laid a hand on his shoulder.

"Listen to Zach," she advised. "It's not like you'll be inconveniencing them. Short of a kitten stuck in a tree, you're likely to be the day's only emergency. Think of it as a favor—you'll be giving the two of them something productive to do with their time."

"Don't argue with Delia," Zach added. "Take it from me—she always wins."

That hadn't come out right. He didn't know why he'd said it. He sounded churlish.

He definitely wasn't over her.

In his youth he'd been devastated by her leaving. Now he was bewildered by her return. Still, he knew he could be handling it better.

"I don't know that *I always win*," Delia countered, her bottom jaw rocking forward as she tempered her response. "But I hope in this case, Spence, you'll take my advice."

Zach was immediately ashamed of himself. He was a changed man now; and, hopefully, a better one, thanks to God's grace. It wasn't like him to bring personal issues into his working life, especially not with a patient present. Seeing Delia again had really done a number on him, much more than he had ever anticipated.

"I guess I'll take that ride, if you're sure it won't be a bother," Spence said, caving in to Delia's persuasive smile.

"That will be best," Delia agreed, patting Spence on the shoulder. "Would you like some help getting out to the ambulance? Morphine can make you a little woozy."

"I'm good." Spence stood and found his balance before gingerly taking a couple of trial steps. Zach hovered at one of Spence's elbows, while Delia stayed next to the other. Her patient was a little shaky, but he appeared stable enough to walk on his own.

"Don't forget to take those pain pills when you get home, Spence," Delia instructed. "The morphine is going to wear off soon and your hand is going to hurt for a while."

"I can't thank you enough, Delia," Spence said.

"I'm glad to be here," she assured him.

Zach's breath caught in his lungs. *Delia* might be glad to be here, but Zach wasn't sure how *he* felt about the fact that she'd so suddenly appeared back in his life.

She had thrown him off balance. Emotionally, he was having a harder time staying upright than Spence was.

He'd imagined Delia's return to Serendipity a thousand times, but the stark reality of the moment was completely different than anything his mind could have conjured—never mind his heart.

"Zach?" Delia called just as he was about to close the door behind him.

Just her saying his name made a ripple of awareness flow through him. He took a deep breath, casually arched an eyebrow and turned toward her.

Her eyes were shaded and her expression neutral. It used to be that he had easily been able to read the depths of her heart through her gaze. But he would have thought the time and distance would have changed that ability.

He was surprised to find that it hadn't. He could see that she was struggling emotionally with this unexpected reunion, just as he was.

He questioned her with his eyes. What did she want—or expect from him, for that matter?

He was aware of the very moment she elevated an emotional barrier. Her gaze turned from a glimmering sapphire to a steel-blue. Clearly, whatever courtesy she had shown him had been for Spence's sake and not his own. Although, why that should surprise him was beyond his comprehension. Hadn't he done the same with her—or at least had tried to do?

He dropped his brow. He didn't know whether she had put their past aside. He only knew that he couldn't.

She had left him without a word. She had broken his heart.

There was so much he wanted, no, *needed,* to say to her, but the words would not come. And even if they had, now was hardly the time.

"Well?" he asked when she continued to stare at him without speaking.

"I just wanted to say thank you," she said in a raspy near whisper that sounded dry and strained.

His brow lowered further. "For what?"

"For helping me out here today. For being there for Spence. I might have been able to do it without you, but I don't think he could have."

"It's my job," he replied curtly.

"Maybe," Delia said, shaking her head. "But I don't think that's all it is."

His mouth twisted but he didn't deny it.

"I'm glad I could help," he said after another extended silence. Help *Spence,* he added to himself.

She hesitated, looking as if she had something else to say, but then her jaw tightened and she shook her head almost imperceptibly. "So, I guess I'll see you around."

He nodded. This conversation was over. His gaze broke with hers as he gestured toward the door. "Spence and Ben are waiting for me."

He turned and nearly sprinted for the door. It was more of a getaway than an exit.

How, he wondered, was he ever going to be able to work with her when just seeing her drudged up so many uncomfortable feelings?

If there was a way out of this, Zach didn't know what

it was. He knew how God would want him to respond—
with forgiveness and love. Zach wasn't sure he could
manage either one of those right now.

Maybe ever.

Chapter Three

Two more days passed before Delia was ready to turn the clinic sign from Closed to Open, and by then it was Friday afternoon and the end of the workweek. The supplies she'd ordered online had arrived and were organized, the financials were up to date. She'd talked Vickie McCall, who'd been Doc Severns's receptionist, into returning to her old job. Monday morning the clinic would officially open for business.

She wondered how long it would be before her tiny waiting room was full of people. The word was definitely out about the clinic reopening, at least to some extent, or Zach would never have known to bring Spence in.

Her best guess was that Jo Hawkins Murphy, the owner of Cup o' Jo, the local café, had learned of her arrival and spread the word. News traveled fast with that good-humored, redheaded lady. Jo was better advertising than a television ad—and a good deal more persuasive—so on the off chance that the woman *hadn't* heard of her return, Delia thought it would be worth a walk down Main Street to fill her in.

Besides, she hadn't had much of an opportunity to reconnect with her old friends—except for the occasional email, and that just wasn't the same thing as face-to-face contact. She was anxious to hear what they'd been up to recently.

Eventually she'd bring Riley along with her and introduce him to the town. She hadn't planned to return to Serendipity, but she was here now and she had to face reality. People were going to start asking questions about Riley. Someone was bound to do the math, and like it or not, the truth would eventually come out.

It was imperative that she protect Riley against the gossip that was sure to arise—and better that she tell Zach the truth before he found it out any other way.

Soon. But not today. Right now, she had enough on her plate just getting the clinic open.

She pulled her hair back into a smooth ponytail and checked her makeup before leaving the clinic. She didn't know why she bothered—Serendipity was a country town with country ways. Hair and makeup were simple here.

Her heavily lined boots clapped loudly against the wood-planked sidewalk as she headed for the café. The ever-present Texas wind had a strong nip to it, and she pulled her wool coat more closely around her neck.

Her mind drifted as she walked. Nothing in the scenery was any different than she remembered from her youth. Serendipity was a settlement unchanged by time, looking nearly identical to what Delia imagined it must have looked a hundred years ago.

It was her perspective that had changed. Her heart. And now she was more confused than ever.

Catching up with old friends and announcing the

opening of her clinic weren't her only reasons for visiting Cup o' Jo. She wanted to know more about Zach before she introduced him to Riley. It was better to be prepared than to be taken off guard, and she'd seen enough in her interaction with him to realize things were different now.

Zach had been a passionate boy, but self-centered in his every thought and action. He'd gotten her into all sorts of trouble—encouraging her to ditch class, driving recklessly with her on his motorcycle—even getting her arrested. It was hard for her to fathom that he could change so completely, even given the ten years since she'd seen him. Leopards could not change their spots, and neither, Delia believed, could Zach Bowden.

Once a troublemaker, always a troublemaker—right?

Still, he hadn't asked if he needed to stay around and help her out with Spence, nor had she indicated in any way that he should have. They both knew it wasn't a paramedic's job to play the nurse, but that was exactly what Zach had done.

Maybe there *was* hope.

As she neared the door of the café, she noticed a man up on a ladder, leaning precariously to one side as he fastened a string of icicle Christmas lights on the eaves with a staple gun. The sun was behind him and she could see only the shadow of his profile, but nevertheless she immediately recognized him—not with her eyes, but with another, deeper sense.

It was Zach.

Her heart lurched into her throat and it took all of her willpower not to turn on her heels and walk the other way. Sure, she wanted to talk *about* Zach and learn more about him, but she wasn't ready to see him again. Not yet.

The only thing that stopped her from fleeing was the very real possibility that he had seen her walking up. But, because of the glaring sunlight, she couldn't tell for sure. He certainly didn't acknowledge her in any way, nor did he stop what he was doing.

Setting her jaw, she moved past him and into the small café without so much as greeting him. Maybe it was best if they ignored each other.

For now.

Delia stepped inside and then stopped, stunned, as she looked around the small establishment. Whereas the town hadn't changed at all, the inside of Cup o' Jo had been entirely renovated. Jo had turned it into Serendipity's own version of a contemporary internet café, with computers lining the back wall and a printer whirring in the corner.

Despite the high-tech upgrades, the homey feeling Delia remembered from her childhood somehow remained. Perhaps it was the mouthwatering smell of fresh pastries emanating from the kitchen.

Jo, her red curls bouncing right along with her ample figure, approached Delia with a vigor that belied her seventy-plus years.

"As I live and breathe. If it isn't Miss Delia Rae Ivers, all grown up and looking just gorgeous," Jo exclaimed in that boisterous but exceedingly friendly way Delia remembered well from childhood. She'd missed the woman, who was like a second mother to her—and to most of the town. "I'd heard you were coming, dear, but how I managed to miss *when* is beyond me. If I'd have known you'd arrived I would've had Phoebe bake you a welcome-home cake."

At the sound of her name, a very pretty and *very* pregnant woman, who Delia guessed to be about her own age, turned from the pastry bin where she was stocking and waved at Delia.

"Phoebe is my nephew Chance's wife," Jo explained. "And as you can see, I'm about to have a grand-nephew or niece." She paused and chuckled. "Or is that great-nephew-slash-niece?"

Jo chuckled and waved her hands. "Oh, well. Whatever. I'm just excited for the baby, no matter what his or her technical relation might be called. I'm ready and waiting to smother the little one with love."

Delia chuckled and nodded to Phoebe. "Congratulations on your baby. You're welcome to stop by my clinic for the rest of your prenatal care if you'd like."

Phoebe smiled. "Thank you. I will."

"But back to you," Jo inserted, making a speed-of-light U-turn to her original subject, "How long has it been now since you've stepped foot in Serendipity?"

Delia realized that the patrons in the café, mostly friends and neighbors from her youth, had stopped what they were doing to see what all the fuss was about. She wasn't shy, so she didn't let it bother her. This was as good a way as any to announce she was back in town and had reopened the medical clinic, even if it wasn't *quite* what she'd had in mind when she'd walked in the door.

"Ten years," said a bubbly, high-pitched female voice from behind Delia's left shoulder. "I ask you, what kind of a friend leaves for *ten years* without even visiting her friends for the holidays?"

Delia turned to find herself wrapped in the animated embrace of her three best friends from high school—Mary Travis, Alexis Granger and Samantha Howell, who were all talking and squealing in turn. There was a good reason the boys on the football team had labeled them the Little Chicks when they'd been freshmen in high school—even now the chirping sound was unmistakable.

"It's good to see y'all," she said, although she knew she'd never be able to express in words how much these women really meant to her. While she'd had friends in Maryland, they were nothing like the Little Chicks. She'd been too wrapped up in medical school and her residency, not to mention single-parenting Riley, to make any truly close connections on the east coast.

"Did you see Zach outside?" Alexis queried, giving Delia's shoulders another tight squeeze. "He's hanging the Christmas lights for Jo."

Her heart dropped into the pit of her stomach and thrashed around in burning waves.

"I…yes. I saw him," she said, hoping that would be enough of an answer to stave off further inquiries.

She wasn't surprised her friends were asking her about Zach. He'd been her boyfriend all through high school. They didn't know the whole story, of course, because she hadn't told them. Other than her parents, she hadn't told anyone.

But she was going to have to tell them, and soon—keeping the most important part of her life a secret was wearing on her. And, at the moment, it was making her feel a little queasy.

"I'm dying of thirst," she said in an effort to change the subject, and thinking maybe a little carbonation would settle her stomach. "Can we get a table and catch up on what's been going on with you? Emailing was nice, but it's so much better to be face-to-face, don't you think?"

Her girlfriends might not have taken the hint, but Jo, who was still hovering nearby, certainly did. The older woman began unobtrusively herding the ladies toward a large table next to the far wall.

"Four sodas coming up," Jo said without waiting for the women to order. "Three diets and one regular."

Delia chuckled. It was exactly the same drink order the girls had made dozens of times in their youth. She was amazed that Jo remembered.

Samantha flashed a mock scowl. "Your figure is as nice as ever," she groused. "I was always jealous that you got to eat and drink anything you wanted without putting on a pound, whereas I couldn't—*can't*—even look at a regular soda without gaining weight."

"You look fine," Delia countered as Jo returned to the table and passed the drinks around. "You all do."

"So when is the clinic going to open?" Mary asked. "Old Doc Severns hasn't been working for a month. If anyone sprains an ankle around here, they have to drive for an hour to get it looked at."

Delia combed her fingers through the length of her hair, offhandedly massaging her scalp. The vision in her left eye was beginning to blur, a sure sign that she was feeling the start of one of her knock-down, dragout migraines. She couldn't imagine why one would hit her now. She was so happy to be with her old friends. It would be a shame if a headache ruined it for her.

Please, God, not today, she thought, trying to breathe deeply.

Not that she was actually praying to God. She'd left her faith when she'd left her youth. It was just a way of thinking and nothing more. It wasn't as if God, if He was there, had time for her headaches. She'd rather rely on science.

She rummaged around in her purse for her migraine medication and popped a pill in her mouth, following it with a long pull on her soda. The medicine wouldn't stave off the headache completely, but at least it might whittle her migraine down to only one night of suffering. Otherwise she'd be in bed for a week.

"Still having your headaches, huh?" Samantha asked.

"Sometimes," Delia confirmed with a groan. "Unfortunately."

"Stress?" Mary guessed. "I remember the day of senior finals. You looked like you were going to outright faint most of the day."

"I *felt* like I was going to collapse," she assured them. "I can't even believe I passed any of those exams."

"And yet you made it through med school," Alexis commented, tilting her head so that her long blond hair brushed over her shoulder. "How is that?"

Delia sat speechless for a moment, stunned by the revelation. Now that she thought about it, how *was* that, that she'd managed long, sleepless nights during her residency, not to mention her years as a single mom with no support?

Because, she realized, her migraines hadn't been as bad in Maryland, stress or no stress. It was coming back to Serendipity that was the real strain on her nerves, and no wonder. Until all of her secrets were out in the open, she was carrying a tremendous burden inside her heart.

"That Zach," Jo said as she swished forward and stopped at their table. "What a good, kind Christian man he's turned out to be. I don't know what I'd do without him, offering to put up the Christmas lights for me again this year—and then stopping 'round today to fix them up when the wind blew half of them off the eaves. Now that's Christian charity for you. Otherwise Chance would have had to do it, and he's already overworked just cooking for me."

Theoretically, Jo was speaking to everyone at the table, but Delia was well aware that the woman's comments were aimed directly at her.

Everyone looked toward her, yet no one spoke a word.

"That's nice of him," she stated, not knowing what else to say.

"It sure is," Jo agreed with a chuckle. "It seems to me that man does more around the community and the church than anyone else in this town. No matter what or when the need arises, he's always the first to volunteer."

It hadn't escaped Delia's notice that it was the second time in as many minutes that Jo had mentioned Zach's faith.

Bad boy Zach Bowden a man of God?

It was hard to fathom. How ironic would it be if Zach found his faith when Delia had lost hers?

Whether she liked it or not, Zach was going to be a big part of her life. She couldn't ignore that fact forever. And she *had* visited Cup o' Jo to find out more about him.

She supposed it was simply that she was feeling a little overwhelmed. She'd learned far more about Zach in this short time than she'd anticipated.

"All right, all right, enough about Zach already. Gone. Poof. Zip it. No more Zach. I don't want to see him, talk to him or think about him." She chuckled, but it sounded fake even to her own ears.

Suddenly, a chill ran up her spine.

No—that wasn't quite accurate. It wasn't a chill, exactly—more of a burning premonition.

She groaned and pressed her forehead with the palms of her hands.

"He's standing right behind me, isn't he?"

If she hadn't already known it instinctively, she would have been warned by the way her friends' eyes suddenly widened and the way the chatter around the table instantly ceased. Even Jo was quiet.

There was nothing to do but to face him. Her stomach roiled as she turned in her chair and glanced his direction. As she suspected, Zach was standing directly behind her and was staring right at her.

And they had an audience. Nearly everyone in the café was watching them.

In Serendipity, they were as infamous a couple as Bonnie and Clyde. She wanted to roll her eyes. Hadn't anything else scandalous happened in the ten years she'd been gone? It seemed to her that everyone's memories were far too keen where she and Zach were concerned.

Thankfully, it wasn't long before the hum of activity in the café resumed. Jo excused herself to go back to waiting tables, and Delia's three girlfriends spoke in hushed tones to one another. Delia couldn't hear what they were saying, but she could imagine.

If she could have, she would've ignored Zach's presence, just as he had done to her when she'd first entered the café; but she found it difficult to break her gaze away from him. He was stunningly handsome in his trademark white shirt, black leather jacket and blue jeans. He held a black cowboy hat in one hand and was curling the rim with his fist.

A muscle twitched in the corner of his jaw. He tilted his head, his gaze still burning into hers.

Alexis, Mary and Samantha stood and hovered around Delia, nudging her upward until she had no choice but to come to her feet. As if that wasn't enough, she was then not so subtly pushed toward Zach. Her heart raced as she experienced the most disconcerting sensation of being back in high school, with her giggling girlfriends making a scene in front of the boy she liked.

But this was different. She was a grown woman now—and she didn't *like* Zach Bowden. He'd practically ruined her life before, and because he was Riley's father, he'd be a trial for her until the day she died.

Zach dropped his gaze from hers, stepped sideways and planted his hat on his head.

"Ladies," he murmured with a clipped nod. A moment later he was striding out the door and down the road.

Delia was equally distressed and relieved. She didn't exactly appreciate his brushing her off with such callousness—but she wasn't quite ready to talk to him, either. Even though it was constantly on her mind, she still had no idea how to say what needed to be said, nor when would be the best time to do it.

Maybe there was no *best* way to say it—and she was going to have to find the time, even if it was wrong.

How in the world would she find the right words?

Zach, you have a son.

Chapter Four

Zach strode down the street with such a fierce determination to get away from Delia that he was becoming winded and short of breath. Or maybe it was seeing her again that had done that to him. Either way, his head was spinning and his pulse was racing.

He'd done everything he could to put Delia's return to Serendipity from his mind. In the last two days, he had cleaned the leaves out of the gutters of his ranch house, patched up the barn to keep his stock warmer against the cold Texas winter, and cut so much firewood that there was no more room to stack it against the side of the house. But even though he'd been tired and sweat soaked from all the hard labor, he hadn't been able to forget that Delia Rae Ivers was back in town, not even for a second.

And then he had to go and run into her while he was hanging Christmas lights at Cup o' Jo. It just figured.

Even though ten years had passed between them, she'd never left his mind—or his heart. As a teenager, he'd been devastated when she'd left suddenly without a word to him. He wished he could forget the way he'd spent a long, frustrating year acting out his anger and getting himself into increasing amounts of trouble.

But then God had caught up with his wayward life and had changed his heart.

Zach Bowden, the kid who'd gotten straight-A student-council president Delia Rae Ivers arrested and thrown in county jail on prom night in their senior year was now a *reformed* bad boy who had repented his sins and given his heart to God.

But of course Delia wouldn't know that. Nor would she have any reason to believe it.

And why should he care? The best thing for him to do would be to avoid her completely, not that that was an option. He was a paramedic and she was the town doctor. Not a good combination.

Lifting his hat, he combed his fingers through his hair and then jammed it back down again in frustration. Somehow, he had to get Delia Ivers out of his head.

Reaching the end of the block, he turned toward the firehouse, where he'd parked his truck earlier. He wasn't on call today, but Serendipity's annual Christmas party was set to take place at the community center that evening and he had planned to change into his costume at the station.

He'd already helped with the decorations at the center and in wrapping presents for the kids, but he had another role to play tonight—the jolly old elf himself.

He'd been Santa for the past couple of years and he loved every second of it—interacting with the children and seeing their faces light up with hope and glee. Just before presents were handed out, Santa traditionally pulled the wide-eyed children into a circle and reverently shared the story of the nativity and the true meaning of Christmas.

What more could a man ask for?

Especially a single man with no children of his own.

"Hey, buddy," Ben greeted as Zach strode in the door of the station. "What's up? I thought you were off today."

Zach grinned. "I am. I'm just here to change into my suit for the Christmas party tonight."

Ben chuckled and patted his stomach. "Oh, that's right. The big red suit. Ho, ho, ho."

"Cut it out," Zach said, scowling, but he wasn't really offended. So what if the guys at the station gave him a hard time about playing Santa every year?

"I'm just glad it's not me," Ben assured him.

Zach reached into his locker and pulled out the red velvet suit with white trim and held the shirt across his chest as he peered at himself through the small mirror attached to the inside door. The outfit was a good deal too large around the middle, but then it was meant to be. He knew he'd have to stuff a pillow down the front to get the right effect. Fortunately, there were lots of those strewn across the cots in the firemen's bunkhouse.

He wondered if Delia would attend the annual Christmas celebration; and, if so, what she would think of him all gussied up in his red suit.

She'd be surprised, that was for sure. Not that it mattered what she thought. He scoffed.

"Just remember that if I didn't volunteer for this gig, you guys would be drawing straws to do the honors," he reminded his coworker jauntily. "Serendipity has been relying on men from the fire station to play Santa for years. You wouldn't want to upset their tradition now, would you?"

Ben held up his hands and shook his head. "Red isn't my color."

"I didn't think so." Zach chuckled. "Are you planning on coming to the party?"

"Are you kidding? I wouldn't miss it for the world," Ben assured him. "I get really tired of my own cooking."

"Tell me about it," Zach groaned as he slid his legs into the downy costume. Bachelor fare was nothing to rave about on his best days, and, like Ben, he wasn't much of a cook. Mostly, he ate whatever he could scoop out of a can or pop into the microwave.

"Let me help you with that," Ben offered when the wide black belt Zach was trying to draw around his waist twisted in the back. It was next to impossible to hold the fluffy feather pillow to his stomach and latch the belt at the same time, so he was grateful for the assistance.

"Well, you definitely look the part," Ben complimented as he stepped back to view his own handiwork. "All you need is to gray up your eyebrows and put on your beard and you're good to go."

"I'm not getting anywhere near that beard until the last possible moment," Zach said, scratching his cheek at the very thought of it. "It itches something fierce."

Ben laughed and shook his head. "Why do you torture yourself?"

Zach grinned. The answer to that question was easy.

"For the kids, Ben. Only for the kids."

Tonight was the night. Her whole life was about to change—not to mention what this would do to Zach and Riley.

It was bad enough running into Zach at the café, but now she had to face him this evening. She couldn't avoid it any longer. Tonight, Delia would tell Zach the truth about his son.

What other option did she have? She couldn't turn back now. She'd made the decision to move back to Serendipity to be here for her mother, who was now wheelchair bound with multiple sclerosis. There was no way she could keep Zach from finding out about Riley. So far, she'd managed to keep Riley's presence a secret from the town, but she couldn't sequester him at his grandparents' house forever—and he was bound to put the pieces together sooner or later. Better he learn the truth from her.

If things went well, and she fervently hoped that they would, she might even be able to introduce Riley to his dad.

And if the opposite happened, if Zach was furious with her for keeping Riley a secret from him—or worse, wanted nothing to do with his son at all—at least they would be in a public place where he couldn't blow up at her and make a scene.

"I understand that Santa Claus visits the party," she told Riley as they drove the short distance to the community center. They were alone in the car. Her mother's multiple sclerosis was flaring up again and her father had opted to stay home with her, urging Delia and Riley to go ahead and have a good time.

"Mom," Riley protested with a mothers-just-don't-get-it groan. "I'm *nine*. I don't believe in Santa anymore."

Delia chuckled. "Not even if he happens to be handing out presents?"

"Really?" the boy asked, suddenly intrigued. When he turned his head in her direction, a lock of his hair, black like Delia's but shaggy like his father's, flopped into his eyes, which were brown and dreamy like Zach's. Her heart clenched at the sight. Riley looked so very much like his father. She hadn't realized just how much until she'd returned home and had seen Zach again.

"That's what I hear."

"Well, maybe, then." He didn't sound convinced.

"You don't have to visit with Santa if you don't want to, but I think it would be awesome if you did."

He tilted his head at her. "Do other moms besides you say *awesome?* I mean, in Serendipity. Grandma and Grandpa kind of talk like cowboys."

Delia laughed. "They do, don't they? I grew up here, so I don't hear the differences as much as you do. Are you afraid you're going to find things too different out here from what you're used to?"

"I dunno." He looked away, out the passenger-side window. "Maybe, I guess."

"Well, don't worry too much about it. I know you aren't used to Texas accents, but after a while you won't even notice. I promise."

"I guess," the boy said again.

Delia really felt for her son and the changes he'd been so abruptly faced with. It was terrifying to move across the country where you didn't know anyone.

She should know. She'd done that very thing ten years ago. But knowing wasn't necessarily helping, and she wasn't sure how to make things any easier for him.

For what seemed like the millionth time since she'd arrived in town, she questioned the wisdom of her decision to move back home. Would Riley really be better off here in Serendipity, or was she creating more problems than she was solving?

"There are plenty of kids in town. I'm sure you'll meet many of the boys your age at the party tonight. It'll be fun to make new friends, don't you think?"

Riley had always made friends easily, which reassured Delia—a little. She was hopeful that he would have little problem finding new buddies to hang out with. If he could make friends before school resumed in January, so much the better.

"It'll all work out for the best," she said, as much for herself as for Riley.

The look he gave her was wise beyond his years. "I know, Mom. Don't worry about it."

Delia wished it was as easily *done* as it was *said,* but she didn't have any more time to think about it because they'd pulled into the community center parking lot. The place was teeming with cars and trucks—mostly trucks, given that the majority of Serendipity's population were ranchers. It looked like everyone in town was here, but then, that was what Delia had expected.

The neighborly, unhurried pace of small-town life was nothing like the frantic, high-octane life she'd been living for the past ten years. And she was somewhat surprised to find she'd missed Serendipity, where a function as run-of-the-mill as the annual Christmas party was the biggest news in town.

As Riley stepped out of the car, he hesitated and glanced at Delia for reassurance. She took a deep breath and smiled at him.

She could use a little encouragement herself. Her stomach was churning uncomfortably as her emotions alternated between nervousness about and anticipation of the night ahead.

"Ready?" she asked as she slid her arm around Riley's shoulders.

He looked up at her and nodded. Her little man. So very brave, putting on a strong game face for his mother's sake.

"We'll just stick together, you and I," she assured him. "We're a team. Just like we've always been."

They were accosted by Delia's old friends the moment they walked through the door. The first to see them was Alexis, who was, naturally, already in the company of Mary and Samantha; apparently, they'd been watching for her.

"Delia," Alexis squealed, darting forward across the crowded room. Her friends flanked her as they approached, making at least as much noise as Alexis.

Delia's grip tightened on Riley and she leaned down to whisper in his ear. "These are the women I told you about. The Little Chicks. My friends from high school. Don't let them frighten you with their prattle."

Riley rolled his eyes.

"Mom," he protested.

"And who is this?" Alexis asked because she was the first to make it to Delia's side.

"This," Delia answered proudly, "is my son, Riley."

All three women started talking at once, addressing questions and exclamations not only to Delia but to Riley, as well. Delia couldn't even tell who was asking what, and she could only imagine how Riley felt.

"How old is he?"

"He's absolutely adorable!"

"He looks just like you, Delia."

"You've been holding out on us. How come you never told anyone that you have a son?"

Delia held up her hands and chuckled. "One question at a time, please. I may be used to your chattering, but you're going to overwhelm the poor kid."

A couple of boys around Riley's age dashed right through the middle of the group, and Riley's eyes lit up with interest. He fidgeted from one foot to the other and looked longingly across the room to where the boys were now swiping sugar cookies from the buffet table.

"Go," Delia said, even though Riley hadn't asked. "Meet some new friends."

"What about you, Mom?"

It warmed Delia's heart to see how concerned her boy was for her. "I'll be fine. These ladies are *my* friends, remember?"

Riley grinned and took off at about the same speed the other boys had been going, somewhere around Mach 3. Delia smiled as she watched him approach the other children. In moments they were all talking and wrestling together as if they'd known each other for years.

Samantha linked arms with Delia and drew her into a corner where it was a little less crowded.

"Dish, girlfriend," she ordered. "And don't leave out any details."

Mary and Alexis had followed, and they both leaned in to hear Delia's explanation, which she *did* owe them. They were her best friends, and she'd said nothing about Riley to them. She felt bad about that, although it had seemed the best solution at the time.

But she couldn't share the whole truth with her friends. Not yet.

Delia looked around the room, searching for that one familiar face, but she didn't see Zach anywhere. For the tiniest moment, it occurred to her that he might skip the party because he knew she'd be there, but she didn't honestly believe that would happen. Zach was too strong willed to let a little thing like having to see an ex-girlfriend whom he happened to dislike stop him from going where he wanted and doing what he wanted.

"I'll answer all your questions, girls. I promise," she assured her friends. "But first things first. Have any of you seen Zach around here? His parents greeted me when I first entered the room, but I've seen no sign of him."

"Zach?" Alexis repeated as her eyes suddenly flooded with suspicion. Her glance flitted to Mary and Samantha, and then back to Delia again.

"Yes," Delia continued. "He'll be here tonight, right?"

"Of course he will," Samantha said. "Didn't anyone tell you? I thought for sure you would already know. Zach is the one playing—"

A deep voice cut off whatever it had been that she was going to say.

"Ho, ho, ho. Merry Christmas!"

Chapter Five

Zach's *ho, ho, ho* nearly turned into out-and-out laughter when he saw the surprised look on Delia's face. Clearly no one had informed her that he'd be the one playing Santa Claus. He immediately decided it had been worth being stuffed into the uncomfortably toasty suit just to be able to see her stunned expression. Her jaw actually dropped.

His eyes met hers and his breath caught in his throat. He wondered if it would always be this way—the current of electricity that zapped him every time he saw her.

Did she feel it, too?

Delia was the first to break away, her gaze flittering somewhere over his left shoulder as if she were looking for someone. Her initial stunned expression vanished as concern worried her brow and set her full, heart shaped lips into a frown.

Curious, he turned in the direction she was looking, but he didn't see anything or anyone in particular that stood out at him. People of all ages were milling everywhere.

Zach's Santa laughter had captured the attention of the children in the room and before he knew it, he was surrounded by little ones clamoring for the opportunity to speak with him and tell him what they wanted for Christmas.

A few older boys were wrestling nearby, trying to look like they didn't have much interest in Santa Claus, but Zach knew better. By the end of the evening they'd all be leaving with one of the gifts he had wrapped and stored in his bag.

Preteen girls huddled in a group and twittered with laughter, reminding him of the Little Chicks, of which Delia had been a part. While the ladies were all grown up now, they were at this moment, with the exception of Delia, clustered together speaking in high tones that still sounded like a flock of birds.

"Ho, ho, ho," he said again in as deep and rich a booming bass as he was able. Santa Claus had a Texas accent. Well, *this* Santa surely did. "Who wants to hear a very special story?"

The children knew what to expect next, and they followed Zach to the middle of the large room, where he pulled up a chair and waited for everyone to seat themselves on the floor in a circle around him. The older boys and girls sat among the smaller children, and even the adults drew near to listen to the most holy story of the birth of Christ.

Zach opened the Bible he'd brought with him and silently waited for the ruckus to die down and for the anticipation in the room to build. He wasn't much of a reader, especially not out loud and to a crowd; but this night was his one exception to the rule.

Unconsciously, his gaze searched for Delia, finding

her at the outskirts of the circle with her arm around a gangly black-haired young boy as she bent her head to whisper in his ear. Zach had never seen the kid before. It didn't take a genius to put two and two together.

Or in this case, one and one.

Delia had a son.

He guessed he shouldn't have been shocked by the revelation, but there it was. Just because *he* hadn't had any remarkable relationships with the opposite sex since she'd left town didn't mean that she'd had the same experience. He was struck once again by the realization of how little he knew about her now.

Was she married? No one in town had said anything about her having a husband, and he figured at least her girlfriends would have known about it. He'd been relatively certain she'd moved back to Serendipity alone, but clearly she had her son with her, and he hadn't known about that.

What other surprises waited for him?

The room had quieted, so Zach turned his attention to the reading from the Book of Luke. He liked being able to relate the story of Christ's birth, especially to the wide-eyed children. That it was Santa Claus reading the blessed story only made it that much more meaningful for him and, hopefully, to the kids.

Afterward, the festive crowd turned to the food. Someone had hooked up a computer to a battered old speaker system and traditional hymns and carols pealed through the air, reminding Zach that he had something important to do this evening—other than playing Santa. Nervousness and anticipation flittered at his throat and he swallowed hard.

He looked for Delia in the crowd but he didn't see

her. He wanted to see if he could find her *now,* but he knew he couldn't, not with all the kids waiting for him to hand out presents.

"Okay, everyone. Quiet, y'all," called Jo Murphy, waving her hand in the air. She had the unique ability to be heard over even the noisiest gathering, and people soon silenced. "Time for Santa Claus here to take requests."

"A new car," one of the older men shouted, making everyone laugh.

Jo snorted and planted her hands on her hips. "From the children, Frank. You know better than that. Are you ready, Santa?" she asked, turning to Zach.

Zach knew that to be his cue. With another hearty laugh, he stepped up on a crudely built wooden platform and sat down on the large black leather chair designated as his throne. He grinned in anticipation as the teenage boy and girl dressed up as elves herded the children into a semblance of a line. In the enormous black sack beside him, he had all kinds of goodies to share with the kids, each marked for a boy or a girl by age. It was, of course, the children's favorite part of the evening.

A couple of little towheaded boys crawled into his lap—Drew Spencer's sons, Matty and Jamey. He chuckled in a low tone as Drew tried to coax them to stop squirming long enough for him to take a picture.

"What do you boys want for Christmas?" Zach asked merrily, wrapping an arm around each of them to keep them from wiggling off of his lap.

"A toy fire truck, and a baseball, and a bat, and—" Matty started.

"And a piano, and some coloring books and some

crayons and a big stuffed horsey," Jamey finished for his twin.

Matty's face suddenly fell and his bottom lip jutted out in a pout.

"What's wrong, little dude?" Zach queried gently.

"Daddy said we weren't supposed to ask for a bunch of stuff. He said we're supposed to thank Jesus for what we have and maybe even give some of our stuff away to kids who can't get any presents."

"Well, your daddy is a very smart man," Zach said, winking at Drew. "But there's something in my sack for each of you. Here you go," he said, giving each of the delighted twins a present.

Still squealing, they dashed off, ripping into the paper as they ran, anxious to see what Santa had given them.

Meanwhile, the next child had shuffled up to him. Turning his attention to the boy, Zach found he was staring into the cautious brown eyes of the lad he'd seen sitting with Delia earlier.

Her son.

"Hello there, young man," Zach greeted, patting his knee. "And what's your name?" Out of the corner of his eye, he could see that Delia was watching the scene, but without looking at her directly, he couldn't tell how she felt about the fact that he was meeting her son for the first time.

"Riley," the boy answered. He stepped forward hesitantly and propped himself unsteadily on the end of one of Zach's knees.

"So, Riley, what can Santa bring you for Christmas this year?"

The boy, tilting his head, met Zach's gaze skeptically. Zach had the funniest feeling he'd seen Riley before, even though of course he couldn't have. Maybe it was just that he looked like his mother. His jet-black hair, bow-shaped lips and the high definition of his cheekbones were smaller replicas of Delia's, an observation that produced the funniest fluttering effect on Zach's heart.

"A basketball," Riley mumbled.

"Yeah? You play?" Zach asked enthusiastically, shaking off the sense of uneasiness he was feeling.

"I used to play in a league in Baltimore. My mom says that once we can afford it, she's going to put up a hoop in the driveway at my grandma's house. That's where we live now."

This wasn't news to Zach. He'd found out where Delia was living as soon as he'd discovered she was in town.

"Well, it isn't Baltimore, but we do have a team here in Serendipity," Zach explained.

"Yeah?" Riley's uncannily familiar brown eyes lit up with interest.

"Sure. Tell your mom that she should contact Coach Bowden, and he'll get you signed up for the team."

"Cool." The boy hesitated and then smiled. "It'll be easy to remember that. Bowden is my middle name."

For a moment, the world stopped spinning on its axis. Shock played havoc with time, and it felt like forever before Zach regained the tiniest semblance of a handle on his spiraling existence.

Riley was his son.

Zach's mind careened around nearly as fast as his stomach, which felt like he'd been sucker punched.

In a very real way, he *had* been. A knife in his gut

might have been less painful than the tortuous agony he was now experiencing. His breath had left his lungs in a rush and wouldn't return.

Shock. Anger. Elation. Joy.

Riley was his son.

No wonder he'd felt as if he'd seen Riley before, and it wasn't because the boy shared some features with his mother.

But only now did Zach understand what his mind had, up until this moment, kept just beyond his reach. The reason Riley looked familiar was because of his eyes, his chin, even the texture and thickness of his hair.

It was like looking into a mirror and staring at his own reflection of when he was nine years old, except that his hair had been brown instead of Riley's black locks.

When he'd first seen the boy, it hadn't even occurred to Zach to wonder how old Riley was. He had just assumed the boy was another man's child.

And why wouldn't he?

Delia wouldn't have kept a secret like that from him. She wouldn't have kept him from knowing his own son.

But she had.

She *had*.

How could she have done this to him?

He was still dazed and in shock as he handed Riley a gift from his sack. The boy took off from the makeshift wooden platform and plunged into the crowd. Zach barely noticed as a two-year-old little girl with her thumb in her mouth promptly crawled into his lap.

As his heart and his lungs slowly started functioning again, a depth of anger and resentment unlike anything he'd ever before experienced formed into a tight ball in his gut and began billowing up into his head.

Now he understood what people meant when they said they were seeing red. His blood pressure must have skyrocketed, for his eyesight truly did become a hazy crimson for a moment as he struggled to calm himself.

He choked back the emotions threatening to overwhelm him. This was the worst possible time and place for him to make such a monumental discovery. How could Delia have done this to him—or had she had just that in mind when she'd brought Riley with her tonight? Maybe she hadn't intended for him to put all the pieces together while he was playing Santa. But, surely, she would realize he'd figure it out sometime during the party, when he'd be surrounded by people and be unable to get a grasp on the way she'd just turned his life inside out and upside down.

When had she become so conniving—even cruel?

But no matter what he was feeling, no matter how badly he wanted to scrap the whole Santa thing to find Delia and demand an explanation, he could not—*would* not. The children in line were laughing and joyful. They didn't realize that their Santa had just had the floor crumble out from underneath him.

He wasn't letting on because he wasn't about to disappoint those kids. It took every bit of his self-control and a frantic silent prayer to God for him to be able to turn his attention back to the children. But with effort, he managed—comforted only by the knowledge that as soon as he could slip away and get out of the Santa suit, he would be hunting Delia down to demand an explanation from her.

Not that he expected much from *that* conversation.

He would never, *ever* be able to forgive her for what she had done to him. But one thing was for certain, he was going to make up for lost time with the boy he'd not even known existed.

His *son*.

Chapter Six

Delia knew the exact moment when Zach had recognized the truth—that Riley was his son—and it couldn't have come at a worse time for him. Or for her.

The whole night hadn't turned out even remotely as she had planned. Circumstances were whirling so far out of control now that she had no idea how she could possibly ever make things right again.

Poor Zach.

Poor *her*—because she knew without a doubt that Zach would be coming after her. And when he found her, he would be beyond furious. And rightly so.

The last thing on earth she would have expected would be for Zach to play Santa Claus at the Christmas party. As a teenager he had *hated* all things Christmas and the dreaded goodwill that went along with it. For him to have made such a hundred-and-eighty-degree turn as an adult was almost beyond Delia's comprehension.

Zach playing the role of Santa completely ruined the plans she had made. She'd intended to take him aside sometime during the party and speak to him alone. But, as Santa, he wasn't going to *get* a moment alone, and even if he did, she could hardly drag Santa Claus off for a one-on-one chat.

As if that wasn't bad enough, she'd misguidedly gone to a lot of effort to get Riley to even consider seeing Santa in the first place. At the time it had seemed the right thing to do.

Because she was a single parent, she felt there were many ways that Riley had had to grow up too fast. She'd fought to preserve whatever precious time he had left of childhood, and to her, at least, that's what Santa Claus represented.

If, upon learning the true identity of the jolly old elf, she'd suddenly and inexplicably changed her mind and encouraged Riley to avoid the man, her son would have been suspicious, at the very least. He was a bright boy—he'd know something was wrong with this picture. It might even have ruined his night, when all the other boys his age got gifts from Santa and he was left out.

But the reality of seeing Riley and Zach together for the first time wasn't anything like she'd expected or imagined. For the first few moments, it was just a matter of trying to breathe around the ache in her heart at seeing Riley on his father's knee. Tears immediately sprang to her eyes, but she was too fazed by the sight of her boy with his dad to even bother to brush them away.

And then Riley had said something that had changed Zach's gaze from amazed, to shocked, to angry, all in a matter of seconds. Whatever it was that had been spoken had tipped Zach off to the truth.

Zach's gaze had searched hers out, and she knew

beyond a shadow of a doubt that he saw the truth in her eyes and in the tears sliding unheeded down her cheeks.

It was too late now to change the way things were going down. She might have made some poor choices in her life, but coming here tonight with the anticipation of bringing the whole truth out in the middle of a public venue had, in all likelihood, been the worst one of all. That she had to face him and attempt to put this catastrophe right was an unavoidable fact. But not in public.

She had to leave the party. Now.

"Riley," she said as he darted past her with one of his new friends. "We need to get going."

Riley spun on his heels. "What? No, Mom. Not yet! We just got here."

Delia would have laughed if it wasn't such a dire situation. They'd been there for a couple of hours at least. But Delia knew what her son meant, and her heart clenched. Riley was making new friends, which was exactly what she'd hoped would happen. The party wouldn't be over for at least another hour—more time for him to play with and bond with the boys.

It was unfair of her to ask him to leave early. But what else could she do?

"Delia." Zach's low, rich drawl, almost a growl, came from behind her and caught her unaware. Startled, she gasped for breath and spun around to face him.

Zach had changed out of his Santa suit and was now wearing his trademark blue jeans and white T-shirt. His dark brows furrowed into a straight line and dropped low over his eyes as angry gaze burned into her.

"Zach," she replied, instantly on the defense. Her

heart was racing. He had every right to be angry, but his thundering expression still took her off guard.

Riley stepped in front of his mother, putting himself between her and Zach. Obviously he was aware of the palpable tension between the two adults, and he had always been protective of Delia, maybe extra cautious because it had always been just the two of them against the world.

In Riley's eyes, Zach was a stranger.

Possibly a threat.

"It's okay, Riley. I've decided we don't have to leave right this second. Go ahead and play with your friends."

"We can go now if you want to," Riley protested. "I don't care."

"No, really," Delia insisted. "Go on. Have fun."

His eyes on Zach, Riley hesitated for another moment, but then one of the boys called his name and he was off in a flash.

"You were going somewhere?" Zach asked, his tone hovering somewhere between disapproval and disbelief.

"No, not really. Just back to my parents' place. It's been a long day," she added, and then wondered why she was trying to explain herself. There was nothing she could say that would bring Zach's temper down from boiling point.

"Without speaking to me." Zach moved closer, invading her space and hovering over her like a dark thunder cloud.

Delia shrugged. She was caught in a web of her own making and she knew it.

So did Zach.

He took her elbow and none too sympathetically led her out the front door and into the parking lot, completely ignoring the curious looks their neighbors flashed them. The temperature was below freezing and the wind only made it worse, but Zach didn't seem to notice. His glower didn't let up as much as a fraction. He'd snatched his coat up on the way out, but he hadn't even bothered to put it on, tucking it under his arm instead.

Unconsciously, she shivered, as much from the confrontation ahead as from the icy temperature.

"You're cold." It was a statement of fact made without the least hint of compassion, yet his touch was gentle as he wrapped his coat around her shoulders.

A rush of warmth shot through her, causing her to shiver in a new way. His jacket was thick and soft and buffeted her against the wind, but it was the inherent tenderness in Zach's action that really warmed her.

"Why didn't you tell me?" he demanded as soon as they were well away from the door and any possibility of being overheard. "Riley doesn't know, does he?" Zach asked bitterly.

"No. I'm sorry." She couldn't bring herself to meet his eyes, so she dropped her gaze.

"You're *sorry?*" he roared, stepping forward and hovering over her, invading her personal space. "What does that even mean?"

Delia flinched but she didn't back away. She deserved his censure. She decided right then and there that she was going to let him have his say, even if it meant letting him shout at her. She'd probably have done the same thing if their situations had been reversed.

"I had to protect Riley," she explained, keeping her own voice soft and level.

"From what? His father?" Zach paced like a caged tiger, jamming both of his hands into his hair and raking his fingers across his scalp as he blew out a deep breath. "How could you not have told me, Delia?"

Delia could deal with Zach's anger, but now the tone of his voice had crept from infuriated to wounded, and that she could not bear. Tears burned in her eyes as she searched for the right words, something that would explain her past decisions while at the same time easing Zach's anguish.

It didn't take her long to realize there *were* no words. There were no excuses. The only thing she could do right now was offer her deep, heartfelt apology to a fire-brand teenager who'd grown into a responsible adult.

"I'm sorry," she said again.

Zach glared at her. "Not good enough."

"I don't know what else to say."

"Really?"

Delia shrugged. She didn't know what he wanted—or at least, she didn't know where to begin to tell him what he wanted to know.

"Answer me one question."

"Okay." Her defenses went on red alert.

"Did you know you were pregnant the day you left town?"

"No." She could see his Adam's apple bobbing as he swallowed, and the pulse in the corner of his jaw was pounding rhythmically. She could see he was fighting to rein in his temper.

He shook his head and scoffed. "Unbelievable. You're still lying to me."

His statement hit her like a slap in the face. "No, Zach. It's the truth."

"Well, excuse me if I don't believe you." He scoffed again, then whirled around and stomped off toward his truck.

She'd certainly buried the hatchet between them—right in his back.

Chapter Seven

Zach yawned loudly as he laced his gym shoes in preparation for his coaching duties at the community center. It was winter break, but the kids liked to meet and play anyway; and he didn't have anything else to do with his Saturday mornings, so he usually joined them.

This morning, however, his spirit was lagging. The last thing he felt like doing was revisiting the scene from the night before, where he'd had the shock of his life in finding out he had a son—not to mention where he'd furiously confronted Delia with the issue.

Even though he knew he had every right to be angry, he wasn't exactly proud of his behavior, but his feelings were still too raw to try to figure out what to do about the situation.

If he had his way, he'd crawl back into bed, pull the covers over his head and pretend none of this had happened—except how could he?

He had a son. A *son!*

That was enough to stagger any man. But he also had other people's children waiting on him, a large gathering of young boys waiting to play basketball. Despite how he felt, he couldn't let them down.

He'd spent a restless night trying to put his thoughts and feelings into perspective. He'd prayed and prayed but had acquired no real peace in his heart about anything.

To find out that the only woman he'd ever really loved was a heartless liar was enough to throw any man's life into a tailspin, but to find out that he had a nine-year-old son whom he hadn't even known about—well, it was nearly too much for him to bear.

He stretched his calves in preparation for a run. It was only a mile and a half from his small ranch to the community center, and he hoped the crisp, cold air would clear his head so that he'd be able to coach his boys with at least some semblance of coherency.

Besides, jogging gave him more time to pray.

There were many things he intended to say to Delia. It would be difficult for him to rein in his emotions, not to rail at her for not telling him the truth, to make it crystal clear how hurt he was by her decision not to involve him in Riley's life.

He had so many questions. He couldn't even begin to put them in a semblance of order.

And of course he wanted to spend time getting to know Riley—his *son*.

He'd always wanted a family, but he'd never quite been able to imagine one without Delia. Now he'd learned that they'd been blessed with a child through their love, however misguided their union had been at the time. Joy like he'd never before encountered rushed through him every time he thought about Riley.

How could he not be elated?

At the same time, he felt desolate. Even though the two reactions were at opposite ends of the emotional spectrum. He had missed so many things in the boy's life. His heart ached just thinking about it.

What had Riley looked like as an infant? What was his first word? How old was he when he first picked up a basketball—and who had taught him how to dribble and shoot hoops?

Zach's anger flared once again. *He* should have been the one doing all of those things. A son needed his father. Didn't Delia even think about that when she so conveniently decided he shouldn't be a part of Riley's life?

For a moment, he once again considered calling off the basketball practice. He could say he was sick or something. He certainly *felt* sick.

He groaned aloud and shook his head. He wouldn't do that to his kids. They depended on him.

In any case, as much as he might want to talk to Delia and Riley, this wasn't the time. His emotions weren't yet under control. He needed time to cool off and pray for God's grace to guide him through this mess.

Was Delia praying as well, or had her faith all been a ruse? He remembered back when they were teenagers and the tender, sincere way she'd shared Christ's love with him. He'd made fun of her beliefs. He'd known she hadn't been comfortable when he'd persuaded her to cross the line—he thought that might have been part of the reason she'd left Serendipity.

Anger swelled in his chest and his breath came in heavy rasps. Could it have been more—that she knew she was carrying his child? She'd denied that she'd known, but she'd also kept Riley's existence a secret from him.

He didn't know what to believe.

There were several cars parked in the lot when he arrived at the community center. Dedicated townsfolk were cleaning up after the party. Usually, he would have dropped in to say hi and probably pitch in; but today he didn't really feel like socializing, so he avoided the community hall and went straight to the gym.

The basketball equipment was already out along the sidelines and in order for practice. Several boys of different ages were shooting hoops, while others milled around jostling and teasing each other.

Zach blew his whistle to assemble the team together, and then gave instructions to begin running laps around the gym.

"Zach?" Delia's voice came from behind him and he immediately tensed. The last thing he needed right now was for her to find him, let alone approach him.

And after the way he'd laid into her last night, he hadn't expected her to seek him out anytime soon.

He turned, determined to tell her—politely, if he was able—that he didn't think now was the time to confront their issues. Instead, his eyes lit on Riley, who was standing by her side. Whatever words he'd been about to speak vanished the moment he set eyes on his son.

The boy didn't say a word, but his posture was defensive and his expression wary. Zach suspected Riley thought he was the enemy here.

If only he knew.

His heart clenched at the sight of the young man being so adorably protective of his mother. The two of them clearly had a close relationship.

Riley's gaze was occasionally drawn to the boys playing basketball, and Zach saw more than one wistful look cross over his face, but he stood his ground and shook his head when one of the boys asked him to come play with them.

Riley was a good kid who loved and protected his mother. That only made Zach all the more determined to be the father the boy needed.

But that could happen only after he worked through the issues with Riley's mother, which was apparently going to be now. He wasn't certain he was ready for any kind of confrontation, but there it was.

"I was helping to take down the decorations from the party when I saw you jog up," Delia explained.

Zach nodded.

"I see," he said, even though he didn't. He would have thought she would start running for the hills if she saw him coming.

"This is Riley."

Zach put out a hand. Riley eyed him a moment before reaching out his own hand and shaking Zach's. Zach grinned. His boy had a good, solid grip.

"Good to meet you, Riley."

"Riley, this is Coach Bowden."

Any guardedness in Riley's expression and posture was immediately erased as his face lit up with excitement.

"You play basketball?" Zach asked, even though he already knew the answer from the night before.

He wondered what Riley would think when he discovered that Zach was his father. What would his reaction be then?

"Maybe you'd like to shoot some hoops with the boys," he suggested.

Riley nodded with enthusiasm, and Delia beamed at her son's delighted expression.

Their son.

"I was on a league in Baltimore. I played center."

"Good to hear. As you can see, we have our own squad here, and we can always use another player. We often play other teams from the surrounding areas. Would you like to join us?"

Riley looked to his mother, who smiled and nodded.

"Do you always meet on Saturday mornings?" Delia asked, sounding as if she were just another parent and not the mother of his child. "That would be the most convenient for us, what with school starting up again after the winter holiday."

"Every Saturday from ten until noon." Zach gestured toward the small office attached to the gym. "Why don't we go into my office for a moment and get Riley's paperwork together."

"Of course." Delia blanched at his words, and for a split second, Zach felt sorry for her.

It was obvious from her demeanor that she knew that signing papers for a basketball league would not be the first order of business once they got behind the closed doors of the office. It was no wonder she was apprehensive.

Zach shook his head. Why was he troubled about her feelings?

She *should* be worried. She still had a lot of explaining to do, and he couldn't imagine anything she could possibly say that would justify the actions she had taken with regard to Riley. It would be touch and go as to whether they could even speak to each other about it and stay civil at the same time.

But she had to have known that before she approached him. She'd been the one to seek him out today, not the other way around. She was obviously ready to come clean with her past. Wasn't that the real reason she was here?

Zach blew his whistle and the boys once again gathered around him.

"Some of you guys probably met this dude last night at the Christmas party, but in case you didn't, this is Riley Ivers. He has just moved into town and he's going to be playing on our team. I expect you to welcome him."

Zach didn't think that would be a problem. From what he'd observed the night before, Riley made friends easily enough.

"I will be in my office for a little while speaking to Riley's mother, so I want you all to take turns practicing your free-throws." He pointed to one of the older boys. "Josh, you're in charge."

All of the boys hovered around Riley for a moment, welcoming him to their team and finding out what he knew about basketball, and then they set out toward the far end of the gym to practice their free-throws.

"Shall we?" Zach asked Delia, putting his hand at the small of her back to guide her. As his fingers touched her and the sweet, soft coconut scent of her shampoo reached his nose, he nearly forgot that he was angry with her and that they had an impossibly wide gap looming between them.

If he pulled her just a few inches closer, she would fit perfectly underneath his shoulder, as if they were made for each other. He experienced a deep, physical longing just to wrap his arms around her, kiss her senseless and forget about the past.

But that he could never do.

He'd once believed with his whole heart that he and Delia were meant to be together. He'd believed in lasting love. But that was before she'd smashed his heart into millions of pieces and left him completely alone to try to put his life back together.

Delia stepped out of his reach the moment he shut the door to the office. When she turned to him, there were tears shimmering in her eyes, and his gut wrenched painfully. He'd never been very good at handling a woman crying, Delia especially. It made him feel helpless and out of control, and he didn't like that.

It was, however, a good reminder to him that he really *wasn't* the one in control. He could count on the Lord to get him through this.

He prayed silently, asking God for strength and wisdom—not to mention the ability to keep his temper under control, which was a constant thorn in his side, to say the least. Right now *all* of his emotions were riding just beneath the surface, bouncing around and smacking into each other like bumper cars. He wasn't quite sure which of his feelings would dominate this conversation—and that was what scared him.

Delia took a deep breath and tilted her chin up resolutely, meeting his gaze straight on. "I imagine you have a lot to say to me. I'll answer all your questions, but I want to say something to you first."

Zach folded his arms across his chest and rested his hip against the side of the desk.

"This ought to be good." He couldn't seem to control the sarcastic tone of his statement.

"I just want to say up front that I know I made a lot of mistakes in the past, and I don't blame you for being angry with me. However good my intentions were at the time, I now understand that what I did was selfish and unfair—not only to you, but also to Riley. I initially returned to Serendipity because my mother is very ill, but now I realize that I need to make things right with you."

Zach tilted his head and narrowed his gaze on her. "And how, precisely, do you plan to do that?" he asked drily, his voice cracking with emotion. "You can't reverse the years. I'll never have all of the special experiences you got to share with Riley. You've stolen those away from me."

"I know." She shook her head and bit the bottom corner of her lip. "How many ways can I apologize to you?"

"You can't. Not really. But I want to hear the truth from your own lips. The *whole* truth."

"I don't even know where to begin."

"How about starting with high school. Tell me why you hightailed it out of Serendipity so fast without as much as saying goodbye to me. Did you find out you were pregnant? Were you just trying to get away from me? At the very least, didn't I deserve an explanation? Did I really matter that little to you?"

Her breath caught audibly at his barrage of questions. "You know that's not true. I love—*loved* you."

His chest tightened so rigidly that it left him gasping for breath. "Then why did you leave me?"

"What, you don't remember us getting arrested for

the possession of illegal drugs?" Her voice was laced with bitterness and a hint of sarcasm. "Drugs, I might add, that I knew nothing about?"

She may as well have slapped him right in the face. No one had to tell him that he'd been nothing but trouble to her as a teenager. He wouldn't deny it.

And yet…

"I'll admit that wasn't my brightest moment," he said. "But, in all fairness, it wasn't a total disaster. It didn't turn out nearly as badly as it could have. Don't you remember? I confessed—I told the police the truth and convinced them you had no part of it. They never charged you with a crime."

"No, they didn't, thankfully—I only had the *delightful* experience of spending the night in jail before everything was straightened out." Her voice was so acerbic that it burned his ears like acid. "I was terrified, Zach. *Terrified.*"

Zach sighed. "Yes, and I'm sorry about that. I suppose we both have things to apologize for." He paused thoughtfully as a new understanding washed over him. "And that's why you didn't tell me about Riley, isn't it? Because I was getting you in to so much trouble—more than I knew."

"Partly," she acknowledged. "What would you have done in my place, Zach?" Her brow knit together over her eyes. "When I found out I was pregnant, I was a long way from home and all alone. You had been self-destructing right before my eyes. If I hadn't left when I did, you would have taken me with you—and Riley, too. You stole my heart and then destroyed it. I couldn't let that happen to our son."

"Our son," he repeated softly. It felt foreign to say

the words; yet, at the same time, it was as if it had always been that way. He and Delia were permanently joined together in their son. In a way, Riley tied all the loose ends together. For all these years, Zach had been living with a deep sense of incompleteness, and now he knew why. God had blessed him and he hadn't even known about it.

Regret merged with shame for all he had lost. How different might his life have been if he hadn't been such a careless and irresponsible youth? When he'd first discovered the truth about Riley, he had placed the whole blame on Delia. Now he was seeing the bigger picture.

To move forward with his life, he was going to have to step up and take some of the responsibility for the way things had gone down in the past.

He held his emotions in check for a moment as he tried to look at the circumstances through Delia's eyes—rationally and without judgment. If he was being honest, he partially understood how she thought she was making the best decisions she could—at the time.

All that she'd said about him was true. He *had* been on the road to self-destruction. And he probably *would* have taken Delia and Riley down with him and bankrupted all three of their lives. There was no denying he'd been heading in the wrong direction even before Delia had left. He'd ditched school, gotten into fistfights and had even run drugs for a while. If it wasn't for the Lord rescuing him from himself, changing his heart and turning his life in the right direction...well, who knew where he'd be?

But God *had* found him. And he *was* different—a Christian man, ready to be a father.

A *father*.

Chapter Eight

"Can you at least try to understand where I'm coming from?" Delia asked softly.

Zach stared at her without speaking. His gaze drilled into her. Finally, he shrugged a shoulder. It wasn't exactly the reaction she'd been hoping for, but at this point she'd take what she could get.

She breathed a sigh of relief. At least she and Zach were talking rationally and not yelling at each other. When she'd first seen him jogging up to the community center she hadn't been the least bit sure whether she should approach him; but, in the end, she'd decided their problems weren't just going to go away on their own, so she might as well take the initiative and address them.

Besides, Riley had been asking her nonstop about when he would get to go meet Coach Bowden and join the basketball team. The sport was important to him, especially because he was trying to make new friends.

"So you really didn't know you were pregnant when you left?" Zach inquired, even though she wondered why he bothered asking—*again*. After all, he hadn't believed her the first time.

She looked him straight in the eye, hoping he would see the truth. "No, I did not."

He narrowed his gaze on her, obviously trying to gauge how honest she was being with him. Finally, he gave a clipped nod, indicating he accepted her words at face value. Whether he really *believed* them was another thing entirely, but it was the best Delia could hope for at the moment.

"So when did you find out, then?" he asked in a low, controlled voice that was a strange divergence from his usual honey-rich drawl.

"About a month after I'd left. I probably should have realized I was pregnant earlier than I did, but I was under so much stress that I didn't think about it."

"Why didn't you return to Serendipity once you found out you were carrying a baby? *My* baby," he amended, his brow lowering. "Wouldn't that have been the easiest for you both? To be with your family? Not to mention, me."

She frowned, her shoulders tightening under the emotional strain. "I considered it, but I'd already found an apartment and registered for school. And for the record, there was no easy answer."

She hated that Zach could so easily put her on the defensive. She'd thought—or hoped, in any regard—that she'd be immune to his innate ability to manipulate or charm her.

Unfortunately for her, she'd quickly discovered that time hadn't changed a thing on either count. She was still very much vulnerable to Zach in every way.

And that was probably because she had unresolved

feelings toward him. When she'd left town she had simply—or maybe not so simply—tucked her emotions deep in her heart and never addressed them. Now, many years later, they'd come back to haunt her.

But she couldn't think about that now. She had all she could do just to deal with the present problems. She couldn't let herself become distracted. Not when so much was at stake.

"I assume your parents knew about Riley," Zach stated acerbically.

"Yes, of course."

"And...what? You swore them to secrecy?" he retorted, his face grim. "Who else knew? Am I the only one in the whole town who wasn't aware I had a son?"

"No, of course not," she snapped, discouraged by the tenor of the conversation. But what else could she have expected? "No one knew. Not even my best friends. I didn't *want* anyone else to know. I asked my parents not to say anything. Although I doubt they would have told you anyway. At the time, you were getting into more trouble than ever, and my parents were really worried about how you would react if you found out I was pregnant with your baby. In their opinion you were too immature to be a father."

"And you believed them." Zach's lips twisted and his face colored a deep crimson. "They had no right to judge me."

Delia reached for his hand, but he pulled away. "Don't be mad at them. They were just trying to protect me."

"Right. In their eyes, I was nothing more than the guy who ruined their teenaged daughter."

She lifted an eyebrow and bit her lip to keep from

stating the obvious and making things worse than they already were.

He *was* the boy who had gotten their teenaged daughter pregnant. How could he blame her parents when all they'd been doing was looking out for her best interests?

And Riley's.

"Well," Zach continued, "however they feel about it—how *you* feel about it—the fact remains that I *am* Riley's biological father." He paused and blew out a frustrated breath.

"Yes, you are," she assured him. Riley was most definitely Zach's son. He'd be surprised to learn the whole truth. There had been no other men in her life.

Only Zach.

"What a mess," he grumbled. "I lost out on so much. You never gave me the opportunity to step up for you and Riley. You were all alone and you didn't have to be."

Delia tried to swallow but nearly choked instead. She hadn't been this confused since the day she'd discovered she was pregnant with Riley.

What would have been?

Should have been?

Might have been?

Zach was right. Now they would never know.

"Maybe you and your parents were right about me," he admitted, his voice harsh. "It's possible that I wouldn't have taken responsibility for Riley, or for you, and that I would have run as far and fast as I could in the other direction. I am the first to admit I was pretty screwed up back then."

He shook his head and jammed his fingers into his

hair, making his already-tousled brown locks even more disheveled. "But I was in love with you. And I would have loved our baby—I do love him. I had the right to know about my son, Delia. You should have told me from the first."

"I intended to…eventually. But as the months went on, it became easier and easier to convince myself that it would be better for everyone if I never said anything at all. As hard as it was getting through med school as a single parent, Riley and I survived."

She paused thoughtfully. "As the years passed, the thought of coming home became more and more frightening. So I avoided Serendipity—and you—altogether."

With a sigh, she turned away from him, rubbing a spot on her temple that was throbbing uncontrollably. She was getting a migraine.

Big surprise there.

In some ways she wished she could detain it at least a little while, although she knew how fruitless any hope of that would be. She needed to be able to think straight if she and Zach were going to get through this, but the vision in her left eye was already becoming blurry.

"I'm not here to make excuses, nor am I trying to rationalize my behavior. I'm just trying to explain the facts," she continued. She hoped her voice sounded more composed than she felt.

"Well, here's another fact for you," Zach said, his gaze hard and his jaw tight. The tension in the small room was palpable. "From here on out, I'm going to be part of Riley's life. A big part. I intend to make up for all the years I lost."

Delia drew back emotionally at his cold, rigid demand. Mentally, she tried to regroup. She knew the things she had revealed to him today had to have hurt him, and to keep from showing it, he was lashing out in anger.

She should have expected that. Some things never changed. "I thought that's what we were discussing."

Zach shook his head fiercely. "We're not *discussing* anything. Riley is my son, and I'm going to be a good father to him. *The father he should have had all along.*"

Her throat was so tight that she couldn't speak.

"Do you want to tell Riley, or should I do it?" His gaze was daring her to argue with him. Well, she wasn't going to rise to the bait.

"We should tell him together."

He reached for her arm. "Fine. Let's go."

She jerked her elbow away from him. "Now, wait just a second here."

Delia felt like she was on a roller coaster and she couldn't get off. Zach was moving too fast. He was being too impulsive. Too much the do-it-now-and-think-about-the-consequences-later Zach Bowden.

That was *exactly* what she'd been worried about.

He was merely proving what she'd known all along. Zach didn't think things through before he acted. He might have grown into a quasi-responsible man who liked kids, but birds couldn't change their feathers. Leopards couldn't change their spots.

And Zach Bowden couldn't change who he was deep down—a charming but impulsive man who didn't have to look for trouble for it to find him.

He didn't understand. They needed more time to work out the details, to plan carefully. How could he not realize that they couldn't simply approach Riley and blurt out the truth—not without running the risk of irreparably damaging the boy.

When they told Riley about Zach, they needed to be together and of one mind—not with Zach dragging her along behind him, literally as well as figuratively. Riley's whole world was going to be rocked by this revelation, and he would need all the support he could get—from both his mom *and* his dad.

"Look, I have to go." Apparently he was changing tactics, for he shrugged and flashed her that charming bad boy smile of his, the one he'd used so many times in the past to manipulate her. His magnetic grin still affected her—more than she cared to admit—but if he thought she was going to yield to him on this, he was wrong.

He opened the door to the office without looking back. She hesitated for only a moment before springing after him.

Her heart was pounding and her head throbbing. She'd been making decisions for years without anyone else's help, and she'd done just fine on her own, thank you very much. She wasn't about to be pushed, bullied or charmed into making a costly mistake.

"Zach, wait," she implored, grabbing for his arm but only managing to snag his T-shirt. "Please, just wait."

"What?" he barked as he whirled on her.

In the past she probably would have given in to his glowering scowl, but she was stronger now, and she had to do what was right for Riley.

"I think we should give this more time," she suggested, her soft voice contrasting with his harsh tone.

He shook his head. "I've missed too much of his life

already. It's way past time Riley knew who his father was."

Delia looked into his eyes and suddenly realized it wasn't his temper getting the best of him. It was his pain and frustration at being left out of his son's life for so long that was adding fuel to the fire.

And that *did* move her heart in a way that his surliness or his inherent charm never could.

"I know," she agreed. "You're right. It is time for Riley to meet his father. Just not today."

Zach's brows dropped low over his soulful brown eyes, but at least he didn't outright ignore her plea. She could see he was torn between what he wanted to do and what would be best for Riley. Maybe she hadn't given him enough credit.

"When, then?" he asked after a moment, jamming his hands in his pockets and staring at the floor.

"Soon."

"You have to do better than that," he pressed, raising his gaze. "When, *exactly?*"

"Christmas Day."

As soon as she said it, she began forming plans in her mind. Christmas was this coming Thursday, giving her only a few days to lay the groundwork with Riley and prepare him to meet his father—but it was better than nothing. Maybe she could give little hints and warm the boy up to the idea.

Then, on Christmas Day, eating dinner together, Zach and Riley would have a little time to spend getting to know each other before the big announcement. Or rather, nothing quite so dramatic—more like a quiet explanation.

That she hoped Riley would eventually accept.

"Okay," he answered in a guttural growl.

The word was muttered so softly that Delia wasn't sure she'd even heard correctly.

"Okay?" she repeated.

"Yes. I don't like it, but I agree with you. We shouldn't try to spring this on Riley without first considering the best way to do it."

"Right," she agreed, relief flooding through her. At least Zach wasn't going to go off half-cocked and do something foolish.

"Christmas Day it is, then," he reiterated. "Where do you want to meet, and when, exactly?"

"I know you probably have family obligations with your mom and dad," Delia said, "but I thought maybe I'd plan our Christmas dinner for later in the evening and you could come visit us then."

His mouth twisted in concern. "You're living at your parents' house, right?"

Delia nodded. "For the time being. Until I get my medical practice established."

"Delia, your parents hate me."

Stunned, she took a mental step backward. He was right. Her parents *did* dislike him. Hate was maybe too strong a word, but she doubted if he would be welcomed in their home.

"You have a point," she conceded. "Let me work on it."

Zach shook his head. "I have a better idea. How about if you two come over to my place for supper? Nothing fancy—I'm not much of a cook. But that would give us the opportunity to be alone together, just the three of us. What do you think?"

She wasn't sure Zach would really want to know

what she thought about being *alone* with him. That had very little to do with Riley and everything to do with the myriad of feelings for Zach that she'd never quite put to rest. Her emotions were so volatile that a single spark would have her shooting up in flames.

She had to remind herself that he was talking about the *three* of them together, with the emphasis on Zach getting to know his son and not on rekindling an angst-ridden teenaged relationship that had been doomed from the start. She was fairly certain *that* thought hadn't crossed his mind at all.

Those days were over.

"What time do you want us?" She hoped her voice didn't sound as choked-up as she felt.

"How about five? That way you'll be able to celebrate Christmas with your parents in the afternoon, but it won't be too late for me to spend time with Riley."

Delia closed her eyes for a moment, trying to rein in the sense of fear and foreboding that threatened to overwhelm her. A tremor ran down her spine as she realized how easily this could backfire in her face.

She'd told her son very little about his dad, although it was getting harder and harder to deflect his many questions. Riley could hate her for keeping his father a secret from him. Zach's heart might be broken if Riley rejected him. Her little boy and the only man she'd ever truly loved were both at great risk here.

Thousands of times over the years she'd imagined them meeting each other, but now that it was really about to happen, she was terrified that it would all go wrong.

At five o'clock on Christmas Day, Riley would finally get to meet the father he'd been asking about. Zach would finally get to tell his son the truth.

And Delia stood to lose everything she held dear.

Chapter Nine

Zach flipped the switch on the surge protector and breathed a sigh of relief when the artificial pine tree he'd purchased the evening before began blinking with dozens of glowing multicolored lights. The tree was a pathetic little thing, only six feet tall and dwarfed by the raised ceiling in his living room, but it was the best he'd been able to get yesterday, it being Christmas Eve and all. Despite his best efforts, he hadn't been able to get to the store until then, and he counted himself blessed that Emerson's Hardware still had a tree in stock.

Over the years, he'd hung plenty of Christmas lights for other people, but he'd never bothered decorating his own place when no one would be there to see it but him.

But this night was different.

Tonight his *son* was coming to visit, and he wanted everything to be perfect. The ornaments and tinsel he'd chosen suited *Delia's* tastes—or at least the kind of thing she'd liked back in high school—but that was beside the point.

He wasn't trying to impress her or anything.

As a final touch, he added an angel to the top of the

tree. It was the only decoration that wasn't brand-new, right-out-of-the-box. The angel, in glowing white ribbons with a Christmas-light candle held in a prayer position in front of her, had been his grandmother's. She had passed it along to him just before her death several years earlier.

It was a gentle reminder of family in a house that he was only now realizing could be barely considered a home. There were no creative touches in his living quarters, only sparse furniture, mostly hand-me-downs that others no longer wanted.

He didn't really care what his couch and armchair looked like as long as they were comfortable. He hadn't even bothered to put any pictures on the walls. It had never mattered that much to him.

But tonight he was picturing his home through new eyes—what Delia and Riley would see when they stepped through the door. He'd done everything he could to spruce up the place, given the limited time he'd had since he and Delia had decided to meet here.

He hoped they wouldn't notice how vacant the place looked. Although why he should be embarrassed about something so trivial was beyond him. It had never bothered him before.

Dinner was in the oven—or rather, the microwave— and he double checked to make sure the table was set and ready. Presumably Delia and Riley had already eaten a big meal with her parents—Riley's grandparents—because deli-cooked chicken from Sam's Grocery, boxed mashed potatoes, and heat-in-the-bag vegetables were about the best he could manage. No one had ever accused him of being a decent cook, and he'd never before had guests for dinner, much less for a special occasion.

Moving back to the living room, he paused, tilting his head and stared at the scene he'd created. It seemed to him that something was missing from the picture, and then he realized what it was. Piles of presents for his son wrapped in festive Christmas colors and cheerful bows.

Regretfully, he hadn't been able to do that this year. Riley didn't even know they were related yet.

But, next year, he'd make up for that loss in spades. He'd probably spoil Riley rotten; but then, he had a lot of making up to do.

He did have one present for the boy, but it was too large to fit under the tree, so he'd stored it in the garage. He wasn't even sure Riley would be interested in a present from the man he'd soon discover was his father.

The doorbell rang, startling Zach out of his thoughts. The time had finally come for him to meet his son, or rather, for Riley to meet his father. He stood and blew out a breath, rocking his head from side to side to loosen the tense muscles in his neck.

Stay calm, he coached himself, trying to lessen the quivering inside his belly.

Right. This was only the most important night of his life. What could go wrong?

Riley was the first one he saw when he opened the door. The boy was bundled up in winter clothing and standing at an angle from the door, shifting from foot to foot. Zach guessed he was either freezing cold or too full of energy to stand still. He was carrying a platter of cookies on one arm and a brand-new basketball tucked under the other. The platter wasn't steady and cookies were sliding precariously close to the edge, but Riley appeared more interested in making sure the basketball was secure.

Zach reached for the plate of cookies and popped one of the goodies into his mouth. Chocolate chip—his favorite. He savored the taste for a moment before swallowing. Leaning his shoulder into the screen door, he allowed Delia, who was carrying two loaves of deliciously pungent banana bread, ahead of him.

"Thank you," she murmured as she went by him. Her rich alto voice was tight with tension and she cleared her throat, no doubt trying to conceal her distress from their son. "I thought Riley was going to drop those cookies."

"No problem. Come in, you two. It's freezing outside." Despite his frazzled nerves, Zach couldn't contain his grin at seeing his son. He didn't even try.

And he couldn't help but notice the enchanting blush staining Delia's raised cheekbones, probably caused by exertion or the cold weather.

Either way—*any* way—she was an exceptionally striking woman. A man wouldn't be able to help himself from doing a double take if he passed her on the street. Her maturity only added depth to her. The years hadn't just been kind to her, but they'd also enhanced her natural beauty. Even now, with her enormous sapphire-blue eyes troubled and her brow creased, she was still amazingly beautiful.

"Food in the kitchen," Zach suggested as he closed the front door against the cold chill of a Texas winter.

Riley clutched his basketball in both hands and hung back, obviously unsure of himself.

"What do you think, Riley?" Zach asked, trying to put the boy at ease. "Did you have a good Christmas?"

Zach waited. Delia was equally silent, her full lips twisting thoughtfully.

"Yeah, I guess so." Riley stared down at his feet and nodded.

"He misses his friends," Delia explained softly. "This move has been hard on him."

Zach heard the warning in her voice. She was afraid of the night's outcome. No matter how they presented the facts, it would be difficult for Riley. There was no getting around it.

But they had to go through it to get to the other side—and they *would* get to the other side. He just wasn't sure how.

"Is that your new basketball?" he queried.

"Yeah," Riley answered, holding it up for his coach's inspection. "Santa brought it for me."

"Cool," Zach answered, making a big show of admiring the ball.

"I got these clothes, too," Riley continued. Sporting goods apparently made much higher marks on Riley's Christmas list than a new pair of jeans and a forest-green polo shirt, and Zach could hardly blame him. He wasn't big on clothes, either.

"You look nice, champ," he said, knowing Delia had bought the outfit for Riley and trying in his own way to make up for the boy's less-than-eager response.

"Riley, your video game is in the car. Why don't you go get it while Coach and I get dinner on the table," Delia suggested, shaking her head at her son, and then at Zach.

Riley started for the door and then paused and turned—his gaze moving between his mother and Zach.

What was holding the boy back? He seemed intimidated by the situation—but, then, was that any big surprise? He'd just moved across the country, hardly knew anyone, and he was inexperienced with his surroundings.

And now Zach was just going to add to the burden. *Surprise! I'm your father.*

He prayed for at least the hundredth time that day for God to bless them.

Delia didn't speak as she entered the kitchen and began unwrapping the bread she'd brought. He struggled to find something to fill the stifling silence.

"Should I have bought him a bunch of presents, do you think?" he asked, coming in behind her. "Buy out the sports section of Emerson's Hardware?"

To his relief, she laughed. "Try to buy your way into your son's heart? I really don't think you'll need to do that. He's going to love you."

Zach hoped so—with all his heart. His greatest fear was that just the opposite would happen.

She glanced his way, and he could see by the way her brow creased that she was having the same thoughts he was. Still, she smiled at him reassuringly.

"He will. You're all he's talked about in the last two days. Coach Bowden this, Coach Bowden that. I think he believes you cause the sun to rise and set in the sky."

"I hope not," Zach said teasingly. "I certainly don't want to rank myself up there with God. He's the only One who can create a beautiful sunset."

Delia pinched her lips and looked away. It was the

briefest expression and was quickly replaced by another shaky smile, but it gave Zach pause to wonder.

The door slammed as Riley returned inside. Peeking around the corner, Zach watched as his son shed his jacket and curl up in an armchair, immediately engrossed in his handheld game.

Assured that Riley's attention was elsewhere, Zach turned back to Delia, who was arranging and rearranging the silverware on the table. She didn't look up, even when he cleared his throat.

"What's wrong?" he asked gently. He was curious. That was all. He knew her better than anyone, and he knew when something was bothering her.

"Hmm?" she replied, obviously pretending she didn't know what he was asking. He thought she *did* understand and was deflecting, but just in case, he reiterated the question with additional detail.

"What did I say that upset you?"

"It's nothing."

Nothing? Is that why she wouldn't meet his gaze?

"Delia," he gently pressed.

She sighed. "It's just that—well, I'd appreciate it if you didn't talk about God in front of Riley."

He couldn't have been more shocked if she'd splashed ice-cold water on him. He'd questioned Delia's faith recently, but now they were talking about Riley. It hadn't occurred to Zach that what she believed—or didn't believe—would affect their son.

She didn't want him to talk about God? Zach's faith was as much a part of him now as the breath that filled his lungs. How could he *not* talk about the Savior?

"I'm afraid I don't understand."

She still refused to look at him, so he reached for her

shoulders to turn her around, and then used his fingertip to gently tilt up her chin so she had no choice but to meet his gaze.

"Tell me what happened," he invited, his voice soft but firm. He tilted his head. "I promise I won't judge you, no matter what you say."

She sighed wearily. "Life happened, Zach. Just *life*."

"You were the one who taught me that God is always with us, no matter what the circumstances, and that we can trust Him to see us through our trials."

"Yeah, well, what can I say?" she asked, with a sarcastic edge to her tone. "I was young and naive back then. Things are different now that I've experienced the world and learned what it's like to be truly alone."

Zach couldn't breathe and he couldn't take his gaze away from the pain in the depths of her deep blue eyes. He experienced a sharp stab of—*something*—deep in his chest. He couldn't identify the emotion, or maybe he didn't want to. For the first time since she'd arrived back in town with their son, he was sincerely considering the past through her eyes, and he didn't like what he saw.

"Who did you have with you for support when you were in the hospital? When Riley was born, I mean?" he asked, his voice cracking under the strain of holding his emotions in check.

"No one." She shook her head. "My mother had planned to fly out, but she got sick."

"No friends who could help you?"

"I didn't ask."

She was a proud woman, his Delia. Proud and strong and infinitely stubborn.

Anger and regret pierced through him. If she'd done

things differently, he could have been there to lend her his strength. To allow her to rest for a change, free from shouldering a lifetime of responsibility on her own. Why hadn't she let him be there at Riley's birth to protect her and care for her when she had needed him most?

But she didn't think she needed him. Leaving him out of the equation had been *her* decision, hadn't it? A knot hardened in the pit of his stomach. It wasn't like he'd had any choice in the matter.

"Delia," he started, but then he paused, not knowing what to say.

She flashed him the most counterfeit smile he'd ever seen in his life and turned back to the table. "I confess I bought these cookies from Cup o' Jo. Chance's wife, Phoebe, makes the most delicious baked goods, so I figured you probably wouldn't mind store-bought this time. I would have baked some myself, but I'm still getting settled in at my parents' house and I didn't have time."

So that was it, then. End of conversation. She was not willing to talk about whatever trials she'd endured after she'd left him, or explain to him how it was that her faith had gone so far by the wayside.

Although it bothered him more than she could possibly imagine, he knew her well enough not to press her on the issue. She'd balk for sure—giving her one more reason to stay on the defensive with him.

It occurred to him that maybe the tide had turned in their relationship. Perhaps he would be the one to share his faith with her, just as she'd done with him all those years ago.

But not now.

She'd turned out the figurative Closed sign and locked the door to her heart.

Silently, he prayed for her. Zach might be struggling to forgive her for what she had done to him, but God never turned His back on His children, and He certainly didn't lose them. If only Delia could see that.

"Obviously, I don't mind store-bought anything," he said, giving her time to regroup. "This whole dinner is practically out of a can. Although, now that I'm thinking about it, I always did love your home-baked cookies. Remember when you used to bring me those gigantic chocolate-chocolate chip cookies after school?"

She nodded, but her gaze still appeared distant.

He opened his mouth to continue his one-sided conversation and then closed it. What else was there to say?

"The house looks nice," Delia said. She glanced at him, and he could see that she'd regained some of her composure, although her eyes still looked glassy.

"Thanks." Zach chuckled drily. "You have no idea the trouble I went to, to make my house look a little Christmassy—is that a word? Christmassy? I hit Emerson's up for everything they had left in stock. I didn't have much time, and I've never decorated before."

"No?" She looked surprised. She probably went to great lengths to bring the spirit of the season to Riley. Or at least the secular part of it.

"Nope. I'm usually the only one to see it, so why bother?"

"I'm sorry," she murmured. With a troubled frown, she laid a hand on his arm. "At least this is a Christmas Riley will never forget."

"In more ways than one," he commented softly, thinking of all the evening might hold for them.

"Yes," she agreed, once again averting her eyes. "I imagine Riley is about ready to eat."

Another deflection.

They'd grown so far apart that Zach wasn't sure how he would ever be able to bridge the distance between them. He stared down at her small delicate hand that was still resting on his arm, connecting them physically—but not emotionally, where it really counted.

For Riley's sake, they somehow needed to work through their issues—confront the past and forge toward the future, however painful that might be.

At best, it would be a long, uphill battle. Maybe impossible.

And for Zach, at least, very possibly heartbreaking.

Chapter Ten

"Put your video game away and come eat," Delia told her son.

"Aw, Mom," Riley protested. "Do I have to? I'm right in the middle of level seven and I think I'm going to beat it this time."

Delia kept her smile in reserve, although she was secretly amused. Riley dragged his feet, looking utterly despondent and completely adorable. "We just ate dinner at Grandma and Grandpa's house," he protested under his breath. "I don't see why we have to eat again." He slid glumly into the chair beside her at the kitchen table and tossed his napkin in his lap.

"I have to start the level over now," he grumbled.

Across the table, Zach smothered a chuckle. Delia flashed him a mock scowl, reminding him that he was an adult at this table.

"Don't be rude," she whispered, leaning in close to Riley's ear. "You are a guest in this house and Coach Bowden has gone to a lot of trouble to fix a nice dinner for us."

Zach sputtered. "I wouldn't say a *lot* of trouble.

And it's *definitely* not what I would classify as a nice dinner."

"You are *not* helping," she told Zach, though she was very nearly chuckling herself. She rolled her eyes at him, glad things were feeling a little less tense.

"Right," Zach agreed, his chuckle turning into a full-blown laugh. His eyes met Delia's from across the table. "Let's eat up, Riley. The sooner you get the food off your plate and into your belly, the sooner you can get back to level seven."

That did the trick. Riley quickly grabbed his fork and raised it above his plate.

Zach reached his arm out and stopped Riley from digging into his food. "Let's say grace before we eat, champ," he explained. "God's been good to us and we should thank Him, especially on Christmas Day."

Riley's warm brown eyes widened as he put his fork back down and folded his hands in his lap; but he couldn't have been more surprised than Delia was at this moment.

Zach praying over food? Who was this man and what had he done with the Zach Bowden she had known and loved?

He glanced at her and shrugged as if it were a commonplace occurrence—and maybe it was, for him. Other than saying a grace by rote over the food at her parents' house, she couldn't remember any other situation in which she and Riley had thanked God for a meal.

Her pride reared in insult. Maybe the reason she didn't say grace is because *she'd* been the one putting food on the table, not God. Why thank Him for what she'd worked so hard to achieve?

Zach bowed his head, and Delia reluctantly followed suit, knowing Riley would do the same. The boy looked up to Zach and clearly wanted to emulate him.

"Heavenly Father, we thank You for Your goodness and mercy in our lives, especially for the food You've provided at this table. Thank You for the opportunity for the three of us to spend time together tonight. In Jesus' name, amen."

"Amen," Riley echoed enthusiastically, clearly wanting to impress Coach Bowden. At a nod from Zach, the boy started forking chicken and mashed potatoes into his mouth as if he were ravenous. Although Delia noted that he studiously avoided the vegetables.

She didn't say a word as she picked up her own fork. There was no *amen* in her heart, and all that served to do was make her feel empty and isolated, two emotions that she went great lengths to avoid.

She saw Zach watching her inquisitively, but she ignored him and made sure his gaze never caught hers.

After a moment, she laid a hand on Riley's arm.

"Not so fast, son. You're going to choke if you keep shoveling your food in your mouth that way. And you have to eat your cauliflower or you don't get to leave the table."

"I made it with cheese," Zach commented. "I think it tastes a little better that way." He leaned forward and cupped a hand across his mouth so Delia could not see his lips. "I don't particularly care for vegetables, either," he said in a mock whisper, "but I knew your mom wouldn't let me get away with just serving up meat and potatoes."

Riley barked out a laugh. Zach winked at Delia and grinned at his success with his son.

She smiled at Zach and Riley and shook her head in bewilderment.

"Men," she muttered helplessly.

Zach and Riley beamed at each other as if they were VIP members of a classified boys' club, high up in a tree house where girls were definitely not allowed.

She didn't know how she felt about Zach and Riley getting along. Part of her was glad for her son that he would now have a dad; the other part of her was downright jealous, which was, she admitted to herself, quite petty.

She didn't want to share Riley's affections. But, then again, she'd had his full attention for years. This new situation would take some getting used to. It wasn't as if they were a family celebrating Christmas together.

Actually, it was. Biologically speaking anyway.

The thought gave her a start. *Mom, Dad and their nine-year-old son.* In theory, a family. In practice, she and Zach were barely on speaking terms and shared custody was going to be difficult.

Still, it felt good to forgo her solitary lifestyle for a change, especially at Christmas. She'd been alone one too many holidays, and Zach was being pleasant, so she saw no reason not to enjoy the moment for what it was.

"So I know you play basketball," Zach told Riley as he cut a bite full of chicken. "Any other sports?"

Riley shrugged noncommittally. "A few."

Delia chuckled at her humble offspring. "He plays nearly every sport the school offers, except maybe track," she informed Zach. "Anything with a ball and Riley's on it. He was varsity on all his teams back in Baltimore."

"I see." She expected Zach to be a little bit more enthusiastic about his son's triumph on the sports field; but, to her surprise, he sounded a little discouraged by Delia's explanation.

Zach might not have been much of a jock in high school, but he coached basketball now. So, apparently, sometime in the ten years she'd been gone, he'd learned a little about sports. She couldn't imagine what was bothering him. She tried again.

"He was even voted Most Valuable Player at a couple of the games, weren't you, honey?"

The boy blushed, but Delia couldn't tell whether it was from the praise or from embarrassment at his mother calling him *honey* in front of his coach.

"That's great, Riley," Zach said. He was slightly more animated this time but Delia still thought his voice was strained. "It sounds like there's not much left to teach you. You probably know more about basketball than I do."

A lump formed in Delia's throat as she realized what was bothering Zach. He hadn't been there to watch his son grow up. Someone else had taught Riley how to dribble a ball and shoot a hoop. She put herself in his shoes for a moment. This couldn't be easy on him, realizing all that he had missed.

"He was in the orchestra, too, first trumpet," Delia said, trying to point the conversation in another direction. Hopefully, Zach didn't lead the town marching band, or she was really going to be in trouble, she thought wryly.

Her comment seemed to do the trick, and the conversation drifted in other directions. It wasn't long before the meal was over and Riley was beginning to squirm in his seat. As her son became antsy, the butterflies in her own stomach grew worse, as if they'd grown sharp edges on their wings.

In some sense, it warmed Delia's heart to see the two of them that way, with the father-and-son camaraderie flowing so naturally between them.

It also made her feel guilty. She should have fixed this mistake years ago.

Riley and Zach deserved to be together. Much to her regret, she knew that now.

If only she could go back in time...

Zach appeared to be lingering over his meal as much as Delia was; but both of them knew the boy couldn't be put off forever.

"Delicious dinner, Zach," she commented, setting her napkin down by her now-empty plate. "Almost as good as the real, home-cooked thing."

Zach winked at her, and she drew back a smile at their inside joke.

"Yeah, it was great, Coach," Riley added impatiently, unaware of Delia's veiled allusion. "Can I go play my video game now?"

Zach frowned and appeared to be carefully considering Riley's request.

"Please?" the boy pleaded.

"Put your dishes in the sink, please," Delia instructed more calmly than she felt. "And then sit back down. Zach—Coach—and I need to talk to you about something."

Riley didn't look too thrilled, but he did what she asked—snatching up his plate and glass and tossing them into the sink negligently. When Delia heard what she thought was the sound of breaking glass, she flinched.

"Riley," she exclaimed, aghast with her son's careless behavior. "Be careful with those dishes."

"I didn't break anything, Mom," the boy assured her, reaching out to take the other plates on the table as well.

"It's okay," Zach said offhandedly. "Really."

"It is *not* okay," Delia countered, standing to her feet and gathering the silverware. "We are guests in your home and Riley will behave himself."

Abruptly, Zach sat back in his chair and brushed a hand down his jaw, his gaze filled with anguish.

Delia was confused for a moment before she understood his change in demeanor. She'd blurted out something that had hurt him.

Delia was a guest in his home, but Riley was not. The boy belonged here.

He was family.

"I'm sorry," she apologized softly and for Zach's ears only. "I didn't think before I spoke."

"No problem." Zach's voice was gruff until he turned to Riley. His face lit up with pure pleasure every time he looked at his son. It was clear how much Riley meant to him. Hopefully, Riley would feel the same way about Zach. Given time, she believed he would.

She poured herself and Zach two steaming mugs of coffee and then sat back down at the table. There was a moment of silence as the adults pondered what to say. Riley looked from one to the other of them expectantly.

She caught Zach's eye and gave a brief, affirmative nod.

They couldn't wait any longer. The time had come to tell Riley the truth.

Chapter Eleven

Zach's heart beat wildly in his chest as he stared across the table at Riley, knowing his next words were going to change the boy's world. Taking a deep breath, he laid a gentle hand on Riley's shoulder and waited until he had the boy's full attention.

"I'm sure you're wondering why you and your mom are celebrating Christmas with me here at my house."

Zach paused as Riley nodded.

"Is it because I'm new in town?" the boy asked hesitantly. "Are you just trying to be extra nice to me because I don't know anybody yet?"

Zach shook his head. "No, not this time, champ."

Riley's face fell. "I don't get it."

"Don't get me wrong. I'm glad you moved to Serendipity. You have no idea how much it means to me that you're here." He was quaking inside. He hoped it didn't show on his face.

"I like you a lot."

Riley looked down at his hands, rubbing one thumb on top of the other. "You do?"

Zach exhaled slowly. He'd been preparing himself

for this moment since the night he'd discovered he was Riley's father. But now, that it was here, he wasn't sure how to handle it, how to say what needed to be said.

He glanced at Delia, but Zach didn't think she was going to be much help. She looked like she was about to pass out right on the spot.

This was frightening for both of them. They were hanging on a precipice in a dangerous and delicate position. One wrong step would send all of them tumbling off the edge, including Riley. But the only way to solve this problem was to work through it—let go and hope they all survived the fall.

"Yes, I like you a lot," Zach repeated. He stood and walked around the table to Riley's side and then crouched before him, looking him straight in the eye. "And that's why we're together today. Your mom and I have something important to tell you."

Riley switched his gaze, wide with panic, to his mother. Zach knew the tone of the conversation was getting way too serious for the boy, and it tugged at his heart that he had to put Riley through this.

Riley had been so happy only moments before. Now the boy's shoulders were stiff and his head was bowed. What if everything went wrong?

From the corner of his eye, Zach saw Delia flinch. She looked absolutely dejected and her troubled eyes glistened with unshed tears.

Zach struggled once again to find the words to tell him the truth. He cleared his throat several times before anything coherent came out of his mouth.

"I'm your dad."

The boy's brown eyes, so like Zach's own, widened

to epic proportions, but Zach couldn't tell if it was out of surprise, shock or dismay.

"You're my *dad?*" Riley repeated quietly, but to Zach, it seemed like the statement echoed in the air. The boy's gaze flashed between bewildered and accusatory but met Zach's square-on.

Swallowing around the lump in his throat, Zach prayed with his whole heart that his son would accept him. He was terrified of the possibility of facing rejection—he'd never been so frightened of anything in his life. His heart hammered in his ears.

"You've got it, champ. What do you think of that?"

Riley shrugged, but he didn't try to leave. Zach released the breath he was holding. He felt rather than saw Delia stand and step behind him.

Zach continued in a raspy voice. "I know you must feel very confused right now, and you probably have a lot of questions."

Zach was feeling more than a little disoriented himself. He couldn't even begin to imagine how Riley felt.

"Just remember that your father and I both love you very much," Delia added, her usually rich alto voice scratchy with emotion.

"How come I didn't know?" Angry and hurting, Riley clenched his fists and pounded on the table top. "If you love me, why didn't you tell me before now?"

Zach glanced back at Delia. The question was inevitable, and Delia had to field it whether she liked it or not. Zach had no idea how much—or how little—she'd said about him.

Maybe she hadn't mentioned him at all.

Delia's eyes wet with tears, she nodded, acknowledging that the question would be hers. She held out both hands in a silent plea, but Riley yanked himself backward out of her reach.

"This past year, you began asking me hard questions about who your dad was and why he wasn't with us," she explained softly. "You're growing up, and I knew I couldn't keep avoiding the subject forever. When we moved back to Serendipity because of your grandma, I knew it was time for you to meet your dad in person—and for him to get to know you, too."

She paused thoughtfully, tears flowing unheeded down her cheeks. "I probably should have told you about him a long time ago."

"Why didn't you?" His accusatory words sliced through the air like a blade.

"Because I was afraid."

Zach was stunned by Delia's honesty. He had expected her to deflect, or at least hedge a little. She'd certainly had no problem doing so in the past.

And then after all this time of keeping silent and playing games with their lives, she now answered Riley's questions directly and honestly—even though it had to be terribly painful for her to admit her part in it.

Riley glowered. "Scared of what, Mom? He's my dad."

That was Zach's question, too, and he hung on breathlessly to hear the answer. What *had* she been afraid of?

Him?

Her lips twisted in that funny way she had when she was considering what to say.

"I don't know," she answered at last. "A lot of things, I suppose."

That wasn't an answer. It didn't satisfy Zach, and it certainly didn't satisfy Riley.

The boy crossed his arms and pulled them tight. His stinging gaze moved from Delia to Zach.

"How come you never came to see me in Baltimore?" Riley asked harshly.

Riley had hit the nail on the head, with the pointed side thrust directly through Zach's gut. Zach's heart roared in his ears and he struggled to pull in a breath through lungs that didn't appear to be working.

He couldn't answer Riley's question without making Delia appear to be in the wrong—which of course she was—but Zach saw no sense in turning the knife on her.

Then again, Riley was placing the blame on *him* for not being there.

Zach's gaze snapped back to Delia. Like Riley, she had her arms wrapped closely and defensively around her, and she looked completely miserable.

Guilty might be a better word for the expression on her face.

He couldn't just ignore the tears welling in her deep blue eyes and flooding down her cheeks. This whole situation was all her fault, and yet he wanted to reach for her and comfort her.

That was incomprehensible—and completely insane.

He turned his gaze back to Riley. "I'm sorry for not being there for you," he apologized, his heart about to burst. "I didn't know I had a son."

"You guys...you guys...I—I can't..." Riley stammered, unable to complete his thoughts. He swiped the inside of his elbow across his face. Zach could see he was struggling not to cry.

"Come here, son," Zach said, offering the strength of his embrace as he wrapped his arm around Riley. "It's all good. We'll figure this out—together."

Delia placed one hand on Zach's shoulder and the other on their son's back. For one brief moment, the three of them were united.

And then Riley shook his head in protest and pushed away from the table, knocking his chair out from underneath him.

"No way. No *way*," he repeated. He muttered something unintelligible as he pivoted on his feet and then ran out of the kitchen at full speed.

"Riley," Zach called, feeling frustrated and rejected and at the end of his emotional rope.

"Let him go," Delia suggested softly. Her hand slid from his shoulder to his elbow and down his arm. "Give him some time to process all this, and then I'll go talk to him."

"And say what?" He knew he sounded bitter, but how else was he supposed to feel? He'd just told Riley that he was his father and Riley had responded by running away.

He knew he was overreacting—and overly emotional. Of course he should have expected that Riley wouldn't joyfully accept the news of his parentage the first time he heard of it. What boy would?

His head acknowledged the facts—but his heart, not so much. He felt disconsolate and empty—more than any other time in his life except when Delia had left him all those years ago.

"I don't have any idea what I'm going to say, Zach," Delia said quietly, her eyes once again filling with

GET 2 FREE BOOKS!

HURRY!
Return this card today to get
2 FREE Books
and 2 FREE
Bonus Gifts!

Love Inspired®

YES! *Please send me the 2 FREE Love Inspired® books and 2 FREE gifts for which I qualify. I understand that I am under no obligation to purchase anything further, as explained on the back of this card.*

affix
free
books
sticker
here

❏ I prefer the regular-print edition
105/305 IDL FMQ4

❏ I prefer the larger-print edition
122/322 IDL FMQ4

FIRST NAME	LAST NAME

ADDRESS

APT.#	CITY

STATE/PROV.	ZIP/POSTAL CODE

tears. Her gaze was resolute but her hands were shaking. "He'll come around. I promise."

Zach nodded, but he knew all too well that for Delia, promises were meant to be broken.

"Riley? Are you okay?" Delia slid down next to her son, who was sitting on the floor next to the Christmas tree, his back to the wall and his knees pulled into his chest.

He clenched his jaw tightly but he didn't answer the question, nor would he look at her. Instead, he stared at a spot on the floor by his feet.

Delia sighed. "I know you're angry with me. I don't blame you."

"I don't get it." Riley's voice cracked with emotion as he struggled to hold back tears. "You used to tell me that my father was *not in the picture.* Then we come here and suddenly I have a dad?"

Delia struggled to find the right words. How could she explain the mistakes she'd made, and how she was now struggling to make everything right? It was way beyond what any nine-year-old boy could understand, or should ever have to know.

"Your father and I broke up before you were born," Delia said. That was not exactly the way it had gone down, but it was close enough. "I was upset with him at the time and I didn't want to see him again. Plus, we were out east, far away from Serendipity. I didn't exactly have a lot of free time between going to school full-time and working to put food on the table."

She knew even as she spoke that she could make excuses all day long and it wouldn't begin to make up for the mistakes she'd made. More to the point, nothing she'd just said would matter to Riley at all. If she believed in God, this would have been a good time to pray.

"What's done is done," she said after a painful pause. "As much as I might want to, I can't change the decisions I made in the past. But I do think you can have a good relationship with Zach—with your father—now."

Riley shrugged and his arms dropped to his sides so that he was leaning on his hands. Delia was relieved to see the less-defensive gesture. It meant they were getting somewhere, although she knew it would take a long time for them to sort out all the details—and the emotions.

"Coach Bowden seems like a good guy," Riley said thoughtfully.

"I think so," she agreed, knowing that her deepest fear was that Zach might not be the man he appeared to be. He'd once hurt her beyond repair. She would not let him hurt Riley, too.

"Do I have to call him dad?"

Apparently, Zach had been hovering nearby for a while, although Delia hadn't seen him. She wondered how much of the conversation he had heard. He stepped forward and crouched down in front of Riley.

"You don't have to call me dad until—and if—you are ready to do so, son." Zach paused and tilted his head. "I guess I ought to ask you if you mind me calling you *son*."

Riley's mouth twisted as he worked out his thoughts, a trait he'd picked up from Delia.

"I guess that's okay," the boy said hesitantly.

"This change isn't going to happen overnight," Delia

said softly. "We don't want you to feel awkward or confused."

"We can go as slow as you want to," Zach added in a reassuring tone.

"Can I tell my friends?" Riley sounded a bit less uncertain this time.

Delia's heart lurched at the smile that suddenly lit up Zach's face. It was like a rainbow after a storm. If she'd had any doubts about Zach's intention to be a good father to Riley, they were put to rest now. She could see how important this was to him—how important *Riley* was to him. It was written all over his face.

She just didn't know if it could stay this way.

"You bet you can, champ," Zach agreed enthusiastically, pounding his fist into his open palm.

"But only when you're ready," Delia said, quickly amending Zach's statement. She didn't want her son to feel rushed, no matter that he seemed to be taking the news well.

She was glad Riley was working through the emotions he was experiencing; but there were warning bells going off in her head that she couldn't ignore no matter how hard she tried.

This whole thing was moving fast—too fast. She didn't feel capable of keeping up, even though it looked as if Zach and Riley might be.

"I can't wait to see the guys' faces when I tell them that my father is Coach Bowden."

Zach chuckled. When he turned his head, he beamed his charming crooked grin right at her, and for a moment she forgot to be worried. She even forgot to breathe.

She'd once been desperately in love with this man.

Her heart hadn't forgotten what it was like to feel so fiercely for Zach, even if she'd done everything she could to put it out of her mind.

"I've got an idea," Zach said eagerly. He stood to his feet, all six foot two inches of him, and reached out a hand to Riley. The boy accepted the offer and Zach helped him to his feet.

Zach immediately turned to Delia and offered her a hand up as well, reaching around to support her waist as she rose. He hadn't been nearly this polite as a youth, that was for dead certain—but what *hadn't* changed was the surge of electricity that struck her when their fingers touched.

"How about the three of us go to church together this Sunday?" Zach suggested casually, raising his eyebrows and continuing to smile as if he'd suggested they attend a baseball game or a cookout.

Delia frowned and shot Zach a warning look. They had already talked about this. Hadn't he understood that she preferred for him *not* to talk to Riley about God?

Her gaze locked with his. He was silently pleading with her through his soulful brown eyes. He knew what he was asking, and he was asking it anyway.

"It'll give us a chance to let all our neighbors know that Riley is my son," he noted, tilting his head and giving her his most persuasive smile. "It makes sense, Delia. Everyone will be there."

She sighed. He was right on that count. Practically everyone in town attended services at the community chapel. There wouldn't be a better opportunity to break the news than in church.

People were bound to find out sooner or later. It would be better for Riley if both Zach and Delia were present when they made the announcement so he didn't feel overwhelmed by the well wishes of the good people of Serendipity.

"All right," she agreed reluctantly, "but only with the understanding that this one occasion is the exception, Zach, not the rule."

He met her gaze, his brow furrowing as he shook his head. "I don't get it," he said softly. "There was a time when—"

She cut him off. "The past is the past. I just don't want people to get the wrong impression about us. Let's just keep our focus on Riley, where it belongs. He's who is important here."

Zach frowned but he nodded nonetheless.

"We'd best be going," Delia suggested. She didn't want to talk about church—or God—anymore tonight.

"Not just yet. I've got a present for Riley to open before he leaves."

Riley had definitely been listening to their conversation, because he perked up immediately upon hearing his name. "Really?" He glanced toward the tree and looked confused when he didn't see a gift underneath.

"Well, it's not actually wrapped," Zach explained with a laugh. "It's waiting for you out in the garage."

Zach and Riley whooped and headed outside, but Delia hung back a little bit, giving them a little more room to bond. She heard Riley exclaiming in a high, excited pitch even before she got to the garage door.

"Mom! Mom!" Riley hollered. "I can't believe it. Come see what Coach got me!"

Delia stepped into the garage. Riley was pointing to an enormous box with a simple red stick-on bow on the top.

Zach was standing to the side with his arms folded, a satisfied grin on his face.

"What is it?" she asked as she approached. As far as she could see, there was no picture on the box to indicate its contents.

"It's a basketball hoop for me to put up at Grandma's house," Riley explained, sounding a little bit impatient. "Coach said he'd help me install it this weekend."

"Whenever's convenient for you," Zach added hastily.

"I'm sure we can set it up a time that will work for all of us," she conceded. "But we'll have to ask your grandparents first, to make sure it's okay with them if we put a hoop up at their place."

"If they'd rather you didn't install it in their driveway, we can always set it up here at my house," Zach offered thoughtfully. "Actually, now that I'm thinking about it, maybe we should go ahead and keep it here. I have a large driveway with plenty of room to play, and that way Riley can come over whenever he wants."

"That might be better," Delia said. Playing basketball together would be a great way for Zach and Riley to get to know one another.

"Yes," Zach exclaimed. "What do you say we go out and put your hoop together now? I have floodlights installed on the driveway so we'll be able to see. We should be able to sink a few baskets before you have to leave."

"I can use my new ball," Riley exclaimed.

"You got it, champ. Let's do it."

Delia started to chuckle at their combined enthusiasm, and thought to maybe point out the lateness of the hour, but then her heart clenched and her throat tightened so painfully that it burned to breathe. She had never imagined in a million years that she would ever see Zach and Riley together this way: a father affectionately draping his arm around his son's shoulder as they talked about where it would be best to set up the hoop.

It was the first time since she'd arrived in Serendipity that she felt complete peace about the move. Finally she knew for sure that this was the right thing to do. It had to be. Zach had matured. He would be there for his child. Riley was safe.

Happy, even.

He knew who his father was, and Zach clearly loved him. With time, Riley would learn to love Zach, too. What more could she possibly ask for?

Chapter Twelve

In Serendipity, everyone dressed up for church. Even transitory ranch hands whose clothes had seen better days presented themselves in their Sunday best with their hair slicked back and their sleeves buttoned at the wrist.

The Sunday service was always one of the highlights of Zach's busy week, but today it was *the* highlight—maybe of his whole life. Just the thought of walking into the sanctuary with Riley at his side put a smile on his face.

He really didn't care to make a fuss over his wardrobe, and, in any case, he didn't have much to choose from that would do in church. He grabbed the black slacks he wore at weddings and funerals and the newest white Western shirt that he had, took a brush to his hat and boots and gave himself a clean, close shave. As a finishing touch, he put a little gel into his hair to tame the wild peaks.

When he looked in the mirror, he hardly recognized himself.

"Spiffy," he mumbled quietly and then laughed

aloud. He was even talking to himself. No doubt about it, he was officially losing it.

Over a boy—and Riley's beautiful mother, Zach supposed. His life certainly hadn't been the same since she'd waltzed back into town.

He and Delia had planned for him to swing by her house and pick her and Riley up in his truck. At first, Delia had balked at the idea of him going out of his way—like he cared about a couple of extra miles—and she had insisted that they could meet at the church.

She was pulling away from him again, but he wouldn't let her. Not this time. She might be a stubborn woman, but he could hold his own.

It had taken a good deal of effort, but, eventually, Zach had convinced her to change her plans. She'd had to admit that it would be easier for all of them if they arrived together in one car—plus it gave them the advantage of setting the stage for their big announcement.

As soon as he pulled up at Delia's parents' house, Riley charged out the door. His mother had clearly had a hand in dressing him—he sported tan cargo pants and a forest-green polo shirt buttoned all the way up to the top button.

Zach chuckled at the boy's hair. Delia had clearly had a hand in it, gelling it and slicking it back. Riley's hair might be the jet-black color of his mother's, but that cowlick in the front was definitely Zach's.

There was no doubt about it. Riley was his kid. And, today, everyone would know it—and see it.

Delia shuffled out the front door in heels and a pretty royal blue dress that complemented her eyes. She stole his breath away.

He held open the door for Delia, then got in, made sure Riley was buckled, and pulled away.

"It's going to get a little crazy for us once everyone finds out you're my son," Zach warned Riley as they drove the short distance from the house to the church. "But it's only because they care. They'll each want to be the first to congratulate us. And if they can't be first, they'll try to be the loudest."

"Even my mother is venturing out today," Delia inserted with what sounded like something between a chuckle and a groan. "She said she wouldn't miss this for the world."

"She probably wants to see me crash and burn," Zach muttered. He made it sound like a joke, but in reality it was all too true.

Delia chuckled in earnest. "I think my mother is actually coming around to you."

"Really?"

"I put in a good word for you. She's seen you around church and in town, and she knows you're working for the fire department. And, of course, I've mentioned how kind you are to Riley."

Zach wanted to cringe. He couldn't help but feel a little bit offended at the way her parents had judged him and found him guilty, especially because they hadn't bothered to get to know the man he'd become. Then again, if he was being honest with himself, he had to admit that in the past at least, he'd done more than enough to warrant any censure they directed his way.

Now that he was a father, he was beginning to see things their way. He wouldn't let anyone hurt his boy. Anyone.

"I won't vouch for my father," Delia continued,

lowering her voice and glancing over her shoulder to make sure Riley's attention was on his MP3 player. "He hasn't quite gotten over your being the boy that got his teenaged daughter pregnant. It's a dad thing, I guess."

Zach had to agree.

"But whether he likes it or not, you're his grandson's father. He'll have to accept that eventually."

Zach hoped that was true. To have Delia's parents against him only served to stress him out even more. While he was thrilled to show off his son to the community, he couldn't help but be a little nervous about it—especially now that he was going to be facing at least a modicum of resistance.

"How did *your* parents react?" Delia asked uncertainly.

He laughed. "Are you kidding? They are so happy to have a grandson that they are breaking apart at the seams. I'm warning you right now, they're going to spoil Riley absolutely rotten."

"Do they hate me?"

He glanced at her, seeing the trepidation in her eyes. "No, Delia, they don't hate you. Not even close. They were stunned about the news, I reckon, but they don't blame you for your part in it."

Delia released an audible sigh.

Zach pulled to the side of the road within easy walking distance of the church and turned off the ignition. He'd avoided parking in the church lot so they would have a few more seconds to collect themselves before entering the chapel. But he knew the people standing near the doorways had seen his truck—and Riley and Delia—and the gossip would already be making rounds.

"Ready, guys?" he asked as they exited the vehicle.

Riley gave an energetic nod, but Delia looked peaked and a little bit shaky. Her nerves must be bothering her, and he could relate. He might not be shaking on the outside, but he was definitely trembling on the inside.

He reached for her and wrapped one arm around her waist to steady her. There was apprehension in her beautiful sapphire-blue eyes when she glanced up at him, but she flashed him a reassuring smile that he returned.

They were in this together.

They were both a little anxious, and although he couldn't have explained it, somehow supporting each other made each of them stronger.

"We'll get through this," he said, leaning in as close to her ear as his cowboy hat would allow. His senses went into a tailspin as he inhaled the scent of fresh coconuts from her shampoo. He'd forgotten how much he enjoyed that smell, which he had always associated with a certain blue-eyed beauty.

Feeling especially bold—or maybe a little giddy from the sweet coconut scent—he planted a light kiss on her cheek.

Her eyes widened and her eyebrows rose so high that they disappeared under her hairline.

"What was that for?" she whispered, definitely stunned but surprisingly not looking as offended as he thought she might.

At least, at first she didn't. Then she apparently remembered that they were not alone.

Her gaze darted around frantically as she looked for Riley. She covered her cheek with her hand as if somehow their son would not see the kiss if she hid it.

Fortunately for Delia—and probably for Zach's well-being—Riley had sprinted ahead without looking back.

"Don't do that again," Delia whispered sternly, her voice urgent and low. She increased her pace, moving away from Zach and toward Riley, who was now waiting for them on the front steps of the little chapel.

Zach held back, giving Delia space.

He shouldn't have kissed her. It was a dumb thing to do.

He wasn't even sure exactly how he felt about her. He was angry at her for keeping Riley from him all these years. All he was doing with his thoughtless public display of affection was confusing him and sending her mixed signals.

As they entered the vestibule to the church, several of his friends greeted him or affectionately slapped him on the back. With his busy schedule, he was particularly grateful for Sundays, when he was certain to connect with friends he might otherwise miss. Cody Sparks shook his hand, seemingly oblivious to the fact that Zach had arrived with Delia and Riley. Chance Hawkins, always quiet, only nodded in greeting, but Zach could see the thinly masked curiosity on his face.

As he walked farther into the building, Drew Spencer pulled him aside and fervently shook his hand.

"I can't thank you enough for helping me out the other day," Drew said with a sincere smile.

"Not a problem, Spence," Zach assured him. "Besides, Delia deserves most of the credit. She patched you up. I just drove you there. How's that hand, by the way?"

"It's healing nicely, thanks to you and Delia. I'd like to speak with her and let her know how much I appreciate having a doctor in town," Spence said, looking around. "Do you know where she might be?"

Zach made a quick survey of the narthex. It took him only a moment to locate Delia and Riley—it was like he had an internal sensor on her or something. He could almost literally *feel* her in the room.

"There she is." Zach pointed toward the entrance to the sanctuary, where Delia was talking with her friends. Riley was standing with them, his hands jammed in his pockets. The indifferent expression on his face was priceless, and he fidgeted uncomfortably. "She's with our son, Riley."

Drew's jaw slackened and his eyes went wide in disbelief. In a different situation, Zach would have laughed at his astonished expression.

"Did I hear you right?" Drew asked. "Riley Ivers is your *son*?"

"Yes, sir. I only just found out about it."

"Well, I'll be," Drew muttered. "I guess I should have figured that one out on my own."

Zach chuckled. "You and me both, brother."

"Figured out what?" Jo Murphy, the perpetually cheerful, bouncy-curled redhead who owned Cup o' Jo, interrupted the conversation, looking at both men with open curiosity and not so much as a hint of shame at having eavesdropped.

Jo didn't even try to pretend she hadn't nosed her way into the conversation on purpose, nor did she care if it had appeared that way. She was like a second mother to half the town, including both Zach and Drew, so, in her mind, it was her right and her duty to know everything important—and even trivial—that went on in Serendipity.

Zach didn't mind. Jo was the most kindhearted individual he knew. If anyone would understand their situation, it was she.

Actually, having her overhear their conversation was exactly what he'd hoped for. Once Jo had heard the news, it wouldn't be any time at all before everyone else would know about it. Zach mentally crossed his fingers, praying once again that this would be a seamless—not to mention painless—transition; not only for Riley, but for him and Delia, as well.

That reminded him, she should be here for this.

"Delia," Zach called, gesturing for her. "Come tell Jo the news about Riley."

Riley stayed at her elbow as she started to cross the room. Just as Zach had observed at the Christmas party, the boy looked as if he was trying to shield her from danger. He took his job as Delia's protector seriously. Zach's heart swelled with pride.

Little did the boy know that *he* was soon going to be the one in need of protection. He was sure to be the center of everyone's attention. Neighbors and friends were well-meaning, of course, but that didn't make them any less raucous.

Delia's friends, the Little Chicks, followed her as she slowly moved across the crowded hall. From the gleeful looks on their faces, Delia had already filled them in on the news. As close as those four women had been in high school, it was no real surprise to him that Delia wanted them to be the very first to know.

When Delia finally arrived at his side, Zach put his hand on Riley's shoulder and smiled.

"This is my son," he announced proudly, loud enough for anyone nearby to hear.

"I knew it, I just knew it," Jo crowed, sharing the happy news with anyone who cared to listen.

That was anyone within a two-mile radius. Jo's voice carried like a bullhorn.

First to approach were Chance and Phoebe Hawkins, the chefs from Cup o' Jo—and Jo's nephew and niece-in-law. Zach couldn't help but envy them. They were a happily married couple expecting their first baby together, and Chance had a teenaged girl from a previous marriage. Phoebe was just glowing, and even the usually stoic Chance had half a grin on his face.

Zach was only now beginning to seriously see himself in a family role as a father to Riley.

Chance's teenaged daughter, Lucy, joined the group and squirmed through the throng to get to Riley's side. Speaking loudly so she could be heard over the crowd, she asked him if he wanted to go hang out with some of the kids his own age.

Riley's full lips twisted, and Zach could see just how much the boy wanted to get away. He could hardly blame him. Zach himself was developing a severe case of claustrophobia just standing here in the middle of the group, with everyone's eyes on him and countless people shaking his hand.

Riley glanced up at Delia for permission, and she nodded. A moment later the boy was racing across the narthex at full speed.

"Hey, son," Zach called. "Slow down a bit. We're at church, not a racetrack."

Riley didn't acknowledge him verbally, but he slowed his pace, so Zach assumed he'd heard him.

"Riley is Zach and Delia's son," Jo exclaimed, so

enthusiastic that her red curls bounced along with her words.

As if there hadn't already been enough people crowding around them, now it seemed like the entire population of Serendipity wanted to congratulate them and know more about the exciting news. For Serendipity, an announcement of this kind was front-page news.

"I guessed it from the start," Alexis said, looking very pleased with herself at her own cleverness.

"We've been talking about it since the Christmas party," Samantha added. "The three of us, I mean."

"We wondered when you were going to admit it, Delia," Mary scolded.

Delia's cheeks turned a deep rose. Zach reached for her hand, but she brushed it away. Friends and neighbors continued to hover around them. With so many voices clamoring for attention, it was hard to distinguish one from another.

"What's the big problem, here?" an old, scruffy-faced man grumbled. Deftly, he used his cane to get past the crowd and into the middle of the circle.

"Frank." Zach had known the man since childhood and knew that his apparent gruffness was just his way of dealing with things. "How are you feeling?"

Frank Spencer made an odd growling sound from his throat. "Miserable, that's what I am. Miserable."

Zach's grin didn't falter. The old man was fitter than the proverbial fiddle, at least for being seventy years old. He had the normal complaints for his age—he just complained louder and longer than the rest of them.

Frank turned his attention to Jo. "Now what are you doing, old girl? Stirring up trouble again?"

"I do *not* stir up trouble," Jo informed him.

Zach caught Delia's eye and winked. The obvious flirtation between the older couple was amusing, but he knew if he asked either one of them separately, they'd deny an attraction of *any* kind to the other.

"I was just saying," Jo continued, "that I'm glad Delia and Zach have finally cleared the air. Now we all know Riley is Zach's son."

Jo nudged her shoulder against Delia, hard enough to tip her off balance and into Zach's chest. She clenched her fists across the front of his shirt to stabilize herself, and he instinctively put his arm around her waist to keep her from pitching to the ground.

Jo beamed at the sight of Zach and Delia together. "And don't they make a lovely family?"

Chapter Thirteen

Delia knew Jo Murphy well enough to know this was a setup—Jo pushing her into Zach's arms. It certainly wasn't a coincidence.

And was it really so crucial for Zach to hold her longer than was absolutely necessary? If she didn't know any better, she would think he was enjoying this.

As for her, she was *mortified*.

Inordinately self-conscious, she released the death grip she'd been holding on Zach's shirt and stepped back, brushing a nervous hand down her dress. Her anxiety blasted toward the stratosphere at an alarming rate.

Going to church in and of itself was more difficult than she could have possibly imagined, especially within this little chapel, where she'd enjoyed many hours worshiping and singing and praying when she was young. At one time it had been her refuge, but now it was simply a glaring reminder of all that could have been.

When had she lost her faith? And why did it suddenly matter to her now?

She couldn't shake the feeling that she was missing something. Something important.

And what was up with Zach? He was acting peculiar, as if he *wanted* their neighbors to think they were a couple—or rather, a family.

A *real* family. At one time that had been her dream—*their* dream. Kids, dogs, the whole nine yards. Talk about youthful folly.

She couldn't even go there. *Wouldn't* go there.

Fortunately she was saved from herself—and from the horde of neighbors trying to offer their congratulations—by the chiming of the bells indicating the service was about to start.

She gestured to Riley and he broke away from the group of boys and came to join her.

Zach placed a hand on Delia's back and the other on Riley's shoulder, then herded them straight up the aisle to the front, where he gestured to the second-row pew.

Really?

Delia saw no reason for them to have to sit where everyone could ever-so-discreetly watch them. In fact, she would have done the opposite—sat in the back where she wouldn't have curious eyes drilling into her. She was uncomfortable enough as it was.

But it was too late to change what Zach had done. She didn't want to make a scene, so she slid into the pew with a soft sigh. She had nobody to blame but herself for being caught in this position. If she'd told Zach the truth from the start, maybe things would have been different.

Then again, maybe not.

She struggled to regain her composure. She was not ashamed of the fact that Zach was Riley's father, even if it had not come about in the best way. Come what may, she would get through this, head held high.

To her surprise, she found the service familiar and comforting. It was nice to be home, surrounded by her neighbors. It was wonderful to hear various members of the congregation reading the Word of God aloud. It had been a long time since she'd heard the Scriptures.

Too long.

It was no wonder Zach couldn't understand why she didn't want to attend church, never mind why she would keep Riley from the services. This was part and parcel of life in Serendipity—but it was something else as well.

She settled in to hear the sermon, her hands clasped in her lap. Zach was seated beside her with Riley to his right. He shifted, placing his arm on the pew over her shoulder, almost, but not quite, touching her. But he might as well have been.

Sitting this way, in Zach's arms, it was nearly impossible not to react to him. Would she ever stop responding so strongly to his mere presence?

She didn't know the answer to that question, but she'd have to work out her feelings somehow. She'd be seeing a lot of him, for the rest of her life—not just in their work, but in the shared custody of their child.

As if he sensed where her thoughts had wandered, Zach glanced down at her and smiled briefly before returning his gaze to the pulpit. She also stared forward, although afterward she couldn't have given the topic of the message the pastor had preached if she'd been asked. Instead, she'd been struggling with her feelings for Zach, and the gentle whisper of the Spirit prodding her to remember the grace of God.

After the service, the folks in the congregation generally migrated to the fellowship hall where the church served cookies and coffee. Today was no exception, although people appeared more interested in hearing about Delia, Zach and Riley than they were in eating baked goods.

It was nerve-wracking to be the constant center of attention, even when the people congratulating her were those she'd gone to church with all through her youth. What was really disquieting was that the whole tenor of the conversation sounded more like she and Zach had just had a baby together, rather than having made an announcement about their nine-year-old son's paternity.

Talk about awkward.

Predictably, Riley had taken off with his friends the moment the service was over. Thankfully, he seemed to be fitting in just fine.

Zach was surrounded by a group of men. He'd been a loner in high school, but now he appeared particularly sociable. What a difference ten years could make.

She glanced around but could not see Riley in the crowd. Delia assumed he was outside playing some sport or other with the boys. Being in Serendipity, she felt perfectly safe leaving her boy to run free as he liked. In Baltimore, she'd had to be more cautious.

Actually, she was a little relieved that Riley wasn't here with her. A boy could only endure so many people ruffling his hair.

Lost in thought, it took her a moment to realize that someone had linked arms with her. She turned to find Samantha at her side.

"Looks like you could use a breather," she said, close to Delia's ear so no one else could hear her. "Care to use the facilities? Mary and Alexis are out there waiting for us."

"Of course." Relief flooded through her. Count on her best friends to read her mind and rescue at the exact moment when another congratulatory statement might have sent her over the brink and into la-la land.

Samantha gently escorted her from the busy room, taking the heat off Delia by speaking on her behalf whenever they passed anyone. She had mentioned visiting the bathroom, or at least Delia had thought she had, but Samantha went right on past the ladies' room and into one of the smaller rooms used for Sunday school classes.

Sure enough, Mary and Alexis were waiting, and they wasted no time on formalities. Swarming around her, they tossed question after question at her.

"We didn't even know you had a son. How could you not tell us?" Alexis demanded.

"He's such a cutie," Samantha added. "He's the perfect combination of his mother and father."

"And *Zach* is the father. How romantic." Mary sighed.

Delia shook her head vehemently. "Okay, now, let's get a few things straight. First of all, you three are crowding me in a whole lot more than the people in the hall. I'm getting claustrophobic."

There was a cheerful round of sorries, but none of the women moved an inch.

Delia took a deep breath and shook her head. "I didn't tell *anyone* about Riley. My parents were the only ones who knew about him. Yes, he is a cutie. He is the center of my world. And there is nothing, *nothing* romantic about the fact that Zach is Riley's father."

"Delia," Alexis chided, "this is us you're talking to. We may have been separated by physical distance for years, but our hearts have always been together. You can tell us the truth. It won't go beyond these four walls."

Mary lifted her fingers to her lips and turned them like a key in a lock. Samantha made an X sign over her heart. Alexis just grinned.

"What truth, exactly?" Delia hedged. "When I left Serendipity, I was pregnant with Riley, only I didn't know it. As for why I didn't come back to Serendipity when I learned I was carrying Zach's child? That's complicated. You three more than anyone know how Zach was back then."

"Yeah, a smokin' hot bad-boy," Samantha agreed.

"Emphasis on *bad*," Delia stated with a frown. "Just being around Zach was like playing a game of Russian roulette. He got me into trouble more times than I could count. I was terrified he might do the same to Riley, even if he didn't mean to do it."

She paused. "I couldn't risk what had happened to me to happen to my son."

Her three friends had, surprisingly, grown rather quiet, which was atypical of them to say the least. They each had pensive looks on their faces, as if they were struggling to process what Delia had just told them.

"And I had school to attend," Delia added, once again feeling the need to justify her actions.

As if she could.

"I couldn't become a doctor without going to college first. And then there was medical school. Having a baby changed my heart and my life, but it didn't change my goals—or my dreams."

"But now you're back," Mary, the quietest of the bunch—relatively speaking—said softly.

"Yes. I have my degree and I've realized I can be useful here in Serendipity. Besides, you all know how sick my mother is."

"And Zach is all grown up," Samantha said.

"*Wow* has he grown up," Alexis added, laughing at her own observation.

"Is there a point to any of this?" Delia asked, deciding there was no way to avoid the one question she knew all three women were dying to ask. She might as well face it head-on.

"Of course there's a point," said Samantha.

"Have you seen Zach in his paramedic uniform?" asked Alexis with a mischievous grin. "He's dreamy."

"Really?" Delia shook her head. "That's your question?"

"No!" Mary and Samantha exclaimed, even though Alexis nodded fervently.

"Then the answer is *yes.*" Delia jumped in before anyone else could speak. "I have seen Zach in his EMT uniform. As you pointed out, he is quite good-looking—and I'm very aware of that fact. A woman would have to be dead not to notice."

With that, Delia turned and walked toward the door.

"Wait," Samantha said, bubbling with laughter. "You come back here this instant, girlfriend. That's not the question we have for you, and you know it. Well, it kind of is, but not really." She laughed even harder.

Delia really, *really* didn't think this was funny. She had fallen for the oldest ruse in the book—jumping from the flame into the fire. And, like a sheep to the slaughterhouse, she'd gone willingly.

Suddenly the mass of neighbors offering their congratulations seemed insignificant compared to what her friends were putting her through.

"You want to know if Zach and I are back together," she stated.

It wasn't a question, and she continued before they could jump in to answer.

"No, we are not, and we aren't going to be. We have Riley in common, and that's it. There's too much of the past between us for it to be anything else. Sorry, girls."

This time she headed for the door in earnest.

"But if it were up to you, you'd at least consider it, right?" Samantha called after her.

Delia didn't turn and she didn't answer, at least not out loud. In her heart, she acknowledged what she would never say aloud.

She just might.

Chapter Fourteen

On Tuesday afternoon, while Delia was busy at the clinic, Zach picked up Riley from his grandparents' house and headed for Cup o' Jo. He had spent the previous day in San Antonio putting together what he hoped would be a pleasant surprise for Delia. Now all he needed was Riley's help.

Zach stretched his arm across the back of the booth and grinned at his son, who was sitting across from him eating an enormous cheeseburger with all the fixings. Zach just couldn't stop looking at the boy, drinking in the miracle of Riley's life and thanking God for the blessing of a son with every breath and every beat of his heart.

"How's the cheeseburger?" Zach asked with a laugh. Riley hadn't said a word since his meal had been placed in front of him.

"Great," he mumbled around a mouth full of food.

"Cup o' Jo serves up mighty fine meals," Zach agreed.

Riley nodded so vigorously that a lock of his hair fell over his brow.

"Are you looking forward to starting school here in Serendipity?" That was only one of about a million things Zach desired to know about the boy. He was afraid he was going to overwhelm him, pelting him with questions like the rounds out of a machine gun.

As for Zach's query about school, Riley shrugged, then nodded and then shook his head. His lips twisted as he thought of a verbal response, and Zach's heart weaved a loop of its own. Many of the boy's little quirks had been picked up from his mother, and the distinctive twist of Riley's lips was one of them.

"So what is it?" Zach queried with a chuckle. "Yes? No? Maybe?"

"No, not really." Riley lowered his gaze back to his meal. "I don't want to go to school here."

"But you've made friends, right?"

"Yeah, but I miss my old ones. My best friend Justin and I used to hang out all the time. Now we only get to text each other."

Zach had never moved away from his hometown, so he hadn't any experience of what Riley was going through. It had to be tough for a boy, moving clear across the country as Riley had, especially on such short notice. Zach wanted to say something to make his son feel better, but he had no idea what that would be, and he was starting to regret the fact that he'd brought up the subject at all.

"I reckon Justin can come down here for a visit sometime," Zach suggested, tapping his fingers on the table. "Would you like that?"

"Sure," Riley agreed with a half grin that was definitely a mirror image of Zach's.

"You'll be all right, son," Zach assured him.

Riley nodded, but he still looked skeptical.

Zach knew there was no reassuring the boy beyond simply allowing Riley time to adjust to his new home. He bit into his own sandwich and the two of them were silent for a few minutes as they ate.

When their meal was over and Jo had cleared the dishes from their table, Zach leaned forward on his elbows, his hands clasped against the smooth laminate tabletop.

"Do you want some dessert, champ? Maybe a slice of pie or a brownie?"

Riley shook his head. "I'm full."

"All right, then. We'll get you some cookies to go and you can eat them later."

"Cool."

Jo, her red curls bouncing and a T-shirt boasting "Pray, *Cook,* Love," bustled over to the table with a white paper bag, which she set in front of Riley.

"There you are, dear. Cookies, hot out of the oven and compliments of the house. I hope you like chocolate chip."

Riley nodded enthusiastically.

Zach chuckled. "You must have read my mind. I just asked Riley if he'd like to take some cookies with him for later."

"I'm quite adept at that skill, my dear," Jo said, rubbing her hands together. "Only it's not mind reading, it's simple observation, it is. I've been watching people my whole life."

"Well, we're grateful for the cookies, aren't we, Riley?" Zach prodded. It was his duty to coax the boy into a polite response, now that he was a father and all.

Right?

Boy, did he have a lot to learn. This was just the tip of the iceberg, he realized, feeling suddenly inadequate about all of the responsibilities into which he'd suddenly been thrust.

"Thank you, Mrs. Murphy," Riley agreed.

Jo shook her hands forward. "Oh, no, my dear. It's just Jo to everyone around here, even the children."

Riley nodded.

"Are you ready to go, then?" Jo asked brightly.

Zach grinned and nodded, but Riley looked confused.

"Do you remember how I said I needed you to help me out with something, champ?" Zach asked.

"Yeah."

"Well, I need Jo's help, too."

Riley cocked his head. "With what?"

"I thought it would be nice to surprise your mom with something special, just for her. She needs to have a little more fun in her life, don't you think?"

Riley nodded but he looked hesitant, and Zach knew why. Fun for grown-ups was not necessarily fun for kids. Often the opposite was true.

Oh, boy, he thought, cringing inwardly. He hoped this bolt from the blue didn't show on his face. His plans were going all awry and they hadn't even started yet. He thought—*hoped*—Riley was going to enjoy the surprise on New Year's Eve as much as Delia was, but the preparations for the celebration, Zach realized, were going to be pure torture to the poor boy.

"Shall I meet y'all at your house?" Jo asked, oblivious to Zach's inner distress.

"Yes, ma'am," Zach answered, rising to his feet. "We'll see you there."

He dug through his pocket and laid a few bucks on the table for the bill, and then he and Riley headed for his truck.

"What's my mom's surprise?" Riley asked as they drove the short distance from the café to Zach's house.

Zach grinned. "I want to take her to see the Houston Symphony Orchestra on New Year's Eve."

The whole getting-the-tickets-for-the-grand-affair thing was a little more complicated than he'd expected, but he didn't think Riley wanted to hear about it. He'd had to take an entire week of extra shifts to bribe the tickets from Chief. That they'd been donated to the fire station, and no one else had appeared to want them, hadn't seemed to matter.

But it would be worth it, if it was possible that she could see another side of him, how completely God had changed his life.

He hoped.

"If I remember correctly, your mother used to love the symphony. You think she'll like my surprise for her?"

"She likes that kind of music," Riley agreed. "She'll probably want to go."

"I'm glad to hear it. I'd hate to go to all this trouble and then have your mother turn me down."

Riley looked across the cab and just stared at him for a moment, his gaze thoughtful. "She won't turn you down," he said, sounding wise for his age and convinced of his statement. "I think she likes you."

Zach's heart jolted to life at Riley's innocent words.

Delia *liked* him? What did that mean in fourth-grade language?

Maybe he should send her a note.

Do you like me?
Check yes or no.

The thought made him chuckle.

"Why do you need me to help?" Riley asked.

Zach pulled into his driveway and shut off the ignition. Jo's beat-up old green truck was already parked by the curb, and she was standing on the front porch waiting for him.

"Why don't we go into the house and I'll show you?" Zach suggested with a wink.

He greeted Jo and ushered everyone inside. Jo immediately took over.

"Bring out the tuxedos, dear, and let's get started," she announced merrily.

"Tuxedos?" Riley groaned.

"Yeah, champ," Zach told him. "That's part of the surprise. You'll be going with us to the symphony."

"In a tux?" He didn't sound thrilled at all about this new twist in this supposedly nice *surprise*. In fact, he sounded as if he'd just been told he was walking right into a hungry lion's cage.

Zach nodded.

"With a tie?"

Zach crouched down to be eye-level with the boy. "I know how you feel. I hate ties, too. But this is for your mom, to let her know how special she is to us. Think you can handle it?"

Riley exhaled deeply and dramatically. "I guess. If

it's for my mom." He paused. His brow furrowed and he chewed on one corner of his bottom lip. "I don't get it, though. I've been to the symphony lots of times, and I've never had to wear a tux before."

Zach laughed and punched his boy affectionately on the shoulder. "It's for New Year's Eve. Everyone's going to be dressed up, not just us."

"All right," Riley conceded, although he looked none too happy about it. "I'll do it."

"It won't be so bad, will it? Other than the part about having to wear a tuxedo, you like going to the symphony, right?"

"Sure. I play trumpet in school."

"I remember your mom saying that."

"Do you guys have a school band in Serendipity?"

"We sure do," Jo answered for Zach as she approached with a child-sized pair of black pants under her arms. "They're a very talented bunch of young people. You'll fit right in, Riley."

The boy didn't look convinced.

"We'll adjust the slacks first, and then we'll take a look at the shirt." She handed the pants to Riley and shooed him into Zach's bathroom so he could change.

"I hope I bought the right size," Zach commented with a deprecating grin. "Shopping for a child is new to me."

"But it's so, *so* wonderful, dear, isn't it?"

Zach took a deep breath and held it, letting the joy in his heart expand and wash in warm waves throughout his entire body.

"It is wonderful," he agreed, marveling at just how happy he felt right now. God had certainly blessed him.

"They're a little long," Riley commented as he returned to the room.

"That's what I'm here for, dear," Jo responded. She pulled a box of straight pins from her purse and opened the lid. "You just hold still and I'll pin the hems up for you," she said through the pins she was balancing between her lips. "I'll stitch these up tonight and get them back to you tomorrow. You'll look just perfect when you surprise your mama."

"I sure appreciate your help, Jo," Zach commented, smiling at the older woman. "I don't think I could have done this without you. When I got out to San Antonio I realized it would be easier to buy tuxes than rent them, but it sure would have been less of a hassle for you if I'd taken Riley along with me for a fitting."

"Nonsense, dear," Jo replied. "I'm happy to do it. And what I wouldn't give to be a fly on the wall when you and Riley surprise Delia Rae, your being all gussied up and all. She's going to absolutely love it."

"I don't know about that." His voice sounded dry and raspy and he swallowed hard.

He wasn't as confident as Jo was about Delia's reaction to his plans. Doubts plagued him. Was he making a mistake in not telling her in advance? What if she was angry about being caught off guard? He might be taking himself two steps back instead of one step forward in their relationship. He wasn't even certain exactly what he was trying to accomplish.

A pleasant working relationship, he supposed. And a pleasant *co*-parenting relationship. This was a peace offering.

"Of course she'll be pleased," Jo assured him. "Just stay with the plan and everything will work out fine.

Now, you're positive she has a nice cocktail dress in her wardrobe, right?"

Zach nodded. "I talked to her mother and she scouted out Delia's closet for me."

Jo tilted her head and raised one eyebrow. "How did that go for you? Speaking to Delia's mama, I mean."

"Not as bad as I expected," he admitted, his lips quirking. "I ran my plans by her and she agreed that it would be good for Delia to have a little fun. I thought she'd still be angry with me about—well, you know— but if she was, she didn't let on."

Jo squealed and clapped in delight. "I told you everything is going to work out for you, dear. For the both of you. I just know it."

Zach shook his head. There was a long, rocky road ahead of him before *everything* could even begin to work out.

But he was determined to walk that road.

For Riley.

And for Delia.

Chapter Fifteen

Delia knew something was afoot, although she couldn't figure out exactly what it was. Ever since Riley had been out with his father two days ago, she'd caught the boy looking at her funny. Watching her. She couldn't imagine why.

Her mother looked better than she had since Delia had arrived. Not only did she smile incessantly but today she was...*hovering*.

That was the first word that came to Delia's mind when she considered her mother's odd behavior. Mama was tailing her in her wheelchair from room to room like a private detective on a stakeout.

What was up with that?

Her father didn't seem to be in on whatever was on her mother's mind, or else he simply didn't care. He was sitting in his usual place in his worn gray armchair reading a thick, hardbound book and completely ignoring the world around him.

She was in the kitchen finishing the last of the lunch dishes when the doorbell rang.

"You should get that, don't you think?" Mama asked

her from where she sat, her wheelchair pulled close to the kitchen table so she could play solitaire. "You know your father. He gets lost in a book and that's the end of it."

Delia stared at her mother warily. Something weird was definitely going on. She would have answered the door even without her mother's prompting. She hardly needed to be told.

And was that Riley's head peeking out from around the end of the hallway?

Her whole body tensed and her breath clinched. It was as if the world stopped and waited for her to open the door—and she knew why. Apparently, so did her parents and Riley, for whatever reason.

It was Zach.

She sensed his presence even before she answered the door.

What she *didn't* know was what he could possibly be doing here. Even after all of the recent events proving Zach's maturity and change in character, she wasn't sure her parents would exactly welcome him with open arms.

Then again, maybe he was braving the new frontier. He was Riley's father after all. It made sense that he'd be around this house from time to time, at least until Delia could get a place of her own.

"Zach," she said as she swung the door open. "What's going on?"

She *saw* what was going on the minute she laid eyes on him—drop-dead gorgeous in a fine black tuxedo with a slim silver necktie, his hair slicked back and the heart-slamming intensity of his bad boy smile firmly in place. The breath she'd been holding ached and throbbed inside her chest. She'd never been as attracted to a man as she was to Zach at this moment. In all these years, she had never experienced that lightning bolt feeling from any other man.

Only Zach.

He didn't wait for an invitation to enter. He sidestepped her into the house, facing her all the while. As soon as she closed the door, he swept a dozen red roses, encased in baby's breath, from behind his back and thrust them at her.

"Happy New Year," he proclaimed in a pleasant drawl.

Delia reached for the bouquet and inhaled deeply. "Thank you," she replied, "but don't you mean New Year's Eve? The new year doesn't officially begin until tomorrow."

He chuckled. "I'm getting an early start, then."

"I can see that," she said, laughing along with him.

Her dad put down his book. Her mother wheeled into the room from the kitchen. And Riley appeared in the hallway, also dressed in a tuxedo and looking so much like his father that it brought tears to Delia's eyes.

Her pulse was racing and her head was spinning as she struggled to interpret the unspoken implications being thrown at her from every direction. Whatever this was, it was big. And apparently, it involved her whole family. Had everyone been in on this except her?

"Okay, so I have to ask, what's up with the tux?" Her gaze flashed to Riley and then back to Zach. "Er, *tuxes.*"

Zach's grin widened to enormous proportions. "I think I'll let our son answer that question."

Riley fidgeted and yanked at his half-attached bow

tie. "I couldn't get this thing to hook on by myself," he said, instead of answering her question.

"Come here, champ, and let me get that for you," Zach said, crouching down and reaching for the boy's tie. "These things are really hard to fasten together sometimes." When he was finished, he stood and ran his palm over Riley's hair to brush back stray locks.

Delia's heart just flipped right over. Zach was such a good dad, helping Riley with his tie without belittling him for not being able to secure the thing himself.

She crossed her arms and began tapping her right foot. "I'm still waiting for an explanation," she reminded her two handsome men.

Well, one handsome little man. And Zach. He wasn't exactly *hers*.

Riley laughed in delight. "We have a secret," he told her cryptically.

Delia shook her head in bewilderment and chuckled along with her son. "Obviously. So are you going to tell me what it is?"

"We're going to Houston!" Riley announced.

Delia raised an eyebrow, directing her gaze to Zach. "Is that so?"

Zach tilted his head and his lips quirked in amusement. "I managed to get tickets to the symphony, to be exact."

Delia glanced at her son. Why hadn't Riley said anything to her about it? He'd clearly known ahead of time because he was already dressed.

"One minute," she said, bolting from the room. She'd been waiting for the orchestra's new CD to come out for ages. Now she could have Riley and Zach pick one up personally for her and not have to pay for shipping.

Scribbling the title of the CD she wanted on a sticky note, she reached for her purse and dumped the contents on the bed. What a lovely time to discover she needed to clean out her purse. Houston was several hours drive, so she knew Zach must be in a hurry. She sifted through a number of crumpled papers and receipts until she found a couple of twenties.

She was a little bit jealous that they were going without her. And how silly was that? If Zach was taking Riley out somewhere, it was a good thing, right? He needed to spend some quality time with his son so they could get to know each other better, and the symphony had always been one of Riley's favorite places to go on a special occasion.

Of course the same couldn't be said for Zach. He was a down-home country boy from the soles of his boots to the tip of his hat—and that included his taste in music. Unless he'd done a one-eighty since his high school years, he wouldn't be the least bit interested in classical music.

What a thoughtful thing to do for their boy.

And it wasn't as if he had completely left her out of the picture. She might not be attending the symphony with him but he'd brought her flowers, which was quite a nice gesture on his part and thoroughly unnecessary. She had nothing to be jealous about.

And yet she was green with envy.

She couldn't help herself. What an epiphany to discover how fervently she *wanted* to attend the Houston Symphony with Zach and Riley, and how disappointed she was that she had not been invited.

But then, why would she be?

This was about a boy and his father, not about the

reuniting of old high school flames. She needed to get over herself—and Zach. She ought to be thanking God that Zach had turned out to be such a great dad, not milling around wondering what might have been between the two of them had she not left town when she had.

She sighed deeply. She was getting in way over her depth here, and raw, heartrending emotions were riding far too close to the surface.

Still sitting on the edge of the bed, she closed her eyes. She had never been more alone in her life—not even when she was in labor with Riley. And yet—

Why didn't she *feel* alone?

All of her five senses and then some became instantly alert and reached out to the nearly palpable sensations washing over her, that same sense of *Being* that had been following her around for weeks now.

Something was different.

She hadn't been looking for God, hadn't asked anything from Him. Honestly, she hadn't been thinking about Him.

She had, in fact, been running from Him for years.

But starting from the second she'd entered the little chapel last Sunday—or maybe from the moment she'd moved back to Serendipity, God had been once more working in her heart, just as He'd done when she was a teenager.

What a strange time to realize that she wasn't alone. She had never been alone. Her faith had wavered and sometimes failed, but in all that time God had never left her side.

She reached for the peace that had hovered just beyond her reach for all these years. Embraced it.

Dear God, she prayed for the first time in ten years. *Is this what You've been trying to teach me? How stubborn I've been to push You away? Forgive me, Lord.*

Her short, simple prayer had an immediate effect. She could not explain the tranquility that washed over her, but it cleansed and refreshed her and gave her a new sense of hope, something she'd been desperately lacking.

She could face this new dilemma—with God's help. The mountain might still be difficult to climb, but at least now she could see a path to follow.

Her priorities instantly shifted as if they'd never changed at all. Putting God as her focus reminded her just how much she loved Riley and wanted what was best for him, even if what happened to be the best for him was Zach.

"Delia?" Her father peeked his head in the doorway, a deep, menacing scowl making his dark brows a straight, low line over his eyes.

Delia was still trying to reel in her emotions. The last thing she needed was her father coming down on her, but he didn't seem to notice the tears blurring her eyes. "What is that man doing here? Did you invite him?"

She turned her head away so he could not see how broken up she was. Taking a deep, calming breath, she shook her head and wiped her wet cheeks with her palms. "No, I didn't invite him, but he's here to pick up Riley for some special New Year's Eve thing."

Her father thundered into the room. In general, he was a quiet man, calm and well in control of his emotions. This was obviously not one of those times.

"Zach Bowden is not welcome in this house," he roared. "Not now, not ever."

"Dad, he is Riley's father," she countered, struggling to keep her voice even.

"I'm well aware of that, young lady," her father continued, as if she were five years old.

"He's going to have to be here from time to time to spend time with Riley."

"Delia," her father said, his voice strained and edgy. "Honey, he hurt you. I don't think I can ever forgive him for that."

Delia looked into her father's eyes and reached for his hand. At first, all Delia had seen was the sheer anger in his posture and his expression, but now she realized it went much deeper than that. Her father wasn't being an insensitive ogre—he just loved his daughter and wanted to protect her, despite the fact that she was a full-grown adult.

"I understand how you feel, Dad, but Zach has changed. He's not the teenaged troublemaker you once knew. He's proven himself to be a pillar of the community and a good, churchgoing man. You might not see it right now, but he's going to be a great father to Riley. All I'm asking is for you to give him a chance to prove himself. I think that's what God would want us to do."

Her father exhaled and squeezed her hand. "Well, I'll admit you're probably right about how God feels about this situation, but the real question is, how does your mother feel about Zach coming around the house?"

Delia smiled and gave her father a soft kiss on his grizzly cheek. "I haven't spoken with her yet, but I'm pretty sure she approves. In fact, I think she's in on this little surprise today with Zach and Riley."

Her father scoffed. "Of course she would be. The old busybody can't keep her nose out of anything," he grumbled affectionately.

"I love you, Dad," Delia told him, her heart swelling for the older man.

"I'm not promising anything," he warned her, "but I'll do the best that I can." Her father reached for her and gave her an awkward pat on the back. He wasn't a man who showed his affection very often, so Delia knew just how special this moment was.

"Come on," she encouraged him. "Let's send Riley and Zach off in style."

Linking her arms with her father, they returned to the living room. Riley had found a baseball somewhere and was tossing it from hand to hand. Zach was crouched in front of her mother and was deep in conversation with her. They were both laughing as Delia entered the room.

Curious.

She approached Riley and forced herself to smile. "Can you guys do me a favor and purchase a CD for me while you're there?" She handed the sticky note and the two bills to Riley. "I've written down the name of it on this piece of paper. Be careful with the money and bring me back the change, okay?"

Riley looked puzzled. "What? Why? You're coming with us, Mom."

Delia was confused. "What do you mean?"

Zach stepped forward and laid a hand on her arm. "I think our son needs to repeat what he just said to you. And this time, try to listen, will you?" he suggested with a chuckle. "He's right on the money, princess."

"What? I don't understand." Her stomach fluttered

at Zach's casual use of his pet name for her. He'd teasingly called her *princess* all the time when they were kids.

"What's to understand? You're going with us."

Delia thought her heart was going to pound right out of her chest. She'd convinced herself that she was fine with not going. She was at peace about it.

She'd been lying to herself.

"Surprise!" Riley exclaimed.

"I...oh, my...this is..." She couldn't put more than two words together to save her life.

"We're *all* going to Houston. Together." Zach looked smug, and his warm brown eyes were twinkling with delight. "And you'd better appreciate the lengths I had to go to get these for you. I have to put in a whole week of extra shifts just to nab the tickets, but here they are." He pulled three tickets from inside his jacket and fanned them in the air.

"I don't have anything to wear," she blurted, because it was the first coherent thought she had.

Her mother wheeled toward her, smiling in a way Delia hadn't seen since she'd moved back to the house. Her countenance shined with joy.

What a difference she observed in her mama—and it was Zach who had done that.

"I checked your closet when you weren't looking," Mama informed her. "And I happen to know that you own a very striking little black dress."

She looked at her watch. It was almost two o'clock in the afternoon. What were they expecting? For her to nod her head and *poof,* she'd be all dressed up and ready to go?

"How long will it take for us to get to Houston?" she asked, now anxious.

Zach put his hands in his pockets, rocked back on his heels and grinned at her. "A little over four hours. I thought we'd pick up some dinner before the show."

"Oh, my," she exclaimed. "That doesn't give me much time to get ready."

Zach shrugged. "How long does it take to throw on a dress? Five minutes? We can wait."

Aargh.

Clearly he had absolutely no idea what *putting on a little black dress* involved. Sure, it would take five minutes to *throw on the dress,* as Zach had put it, but then there was finding appropriate heels, donning pantyhose and applying *real* makeup and not just the single application of mascara she had on now. After that, there was hair, and perfume, and—

Oh, what was she waiting for? She was going to the symphony with Riley and *Zach!* She gave her mother a pleading look and headed for the bedroom. She would need all the help she could get.

"Back in a flash," she called over her shoulder. Which she hoped would be true, as long as they used a very, *very* relative definition of the word *flash.*

She laughed all the way down the hallway.

Chapter Sixteen

Zach knew he had made the right decision the moment Delia walked out of the bedroom in that gorgeous little black number of hers. It had taken her twenty minutes, not five, for her to get dressed, but the moment he laid eyes on her, he knew it had been well worth the wait.

Beautiful didn't even begin to cover it. Delia simply glowed, reminding Zach of the angel on the top of his Christmas tree. The way she'd applied her makeup made her already-large sapphire eyes appear enormous, and the smile that lit her face said it all.

She was excited. Maybe even happy.

And here he'd been afraid she would turn him down.

Oh—and he *had* been afraid. That was part of the reason he'd ultimately decided to surprise her, rather than give her the opportunity to think about his offer— he didn't want her to be able to say no.

Not that he was trying to force her hand exactly. For his part, he just wanted to prove himself and win back her trust. He just prayed she would give him a chance and not shut him down in his tracks.

He hadn't expected the New Year's Eve traffic to be

quite as heavy as it was, so it took them a little longer to make it to Houston than he'd anticipated. Delia didn't appear to mind. Conversation was abundant and carefree, although they were both careful to stay on neutral topics.

Riley occasionally chimed in from the backseat of the cab, although at first his attention had been focused on his portable video game. Riley had both Zach and Delia in stitches with his childish observations and his pure, innocent excitement about the night ahead.

"You know you'll have to stay up past midnight, right, champ?" Zach asked as he pulled into the drive-through of a fast-food restaurant in downtown Houston.

Riley exclaimed in delight. "I've stayed up late lots of times," he informed his father, sounding offended that Zach didn't think he could stay awake.

"It's a good thing, then, because there's going to be plenty of excitement come midnight."

At least if everything went as he hoped. While some of his plans seemed to be coming off without a hitch, he'd had to modify others. But the members of his *family* didn't seem to care what they did. He sure liked that word. It made his stomach quiver every time he thought about it, which was often.

He'd wanted to treat Delia and Riley to a nice sit-down dinner, but they'd run out of time, more because of the traffic than in his misjudgment of how long it would take Delia to get ready.

Hopefully the symphony VIP after-party would make up for the pathetic little hamburgers and French fries they'd settled for.

Their arrival at Jones Hall was cause for many happy exclamations from Delia and Riley, but nothing more so than when the usher paraded them down to the front row and showed them their seats. He hated classical music, but being sandwiched between Delia and Riley definitely made up for any aural discomfort he might experience.

"I didn't look at the tickets that closely," Delia admitted as she took her seat next to Zach. "I had no idea we were going to have such a good view."

Zach raised his eyebrows in question. What was there to view at a symphony?

Delia laughed as if reading his mind. "I do like to watch the orchestra as well as listen to it. I had no idea we had front row seats. I guess it's just as well—it added to my surprise."

"And the evening gets even better," Zach promised her with a sly grin.

He intended to keep that promise, and show this beautiful woman and the son he'd always wanted—but never knew he had—a night they would never forget.

Next to him, Riley sat restless, tapping one foot and then the other on the hard cement floor. His shiny shoes were already a little bit scuffed. Zach wondered how the boy had managed to do that given the time they'd had.

He chuckled as he leaned toward his son. "It's kind of boring just having to wait, isn't it?"

Riley grinned up at him and nodded. Every time the boy smiled Zach's heart just melted.

Fortunately—or maybe not so much, for Zach anyway—the symphony started. He supposed it really wasn't that bad, especially when he casually slipped his arm around the back of Delia's chair, almost but not quite touching her shoulder, and she didn't try to stop him. Even though he much preferred country music, he could stomach the horns and violins as long as Delia and Riley were near.

Still, he was grateful when it was over. He guided Delia and Riley through the crush and out the door, but he headed the opposite way of where he'd parked the truck.

"Where are we going now?" Delia asked observantly. "Is this another one of your surprises?"

Zach hoped his smile didn't give it all away. "Seriously? You can't believe that listening to those violins squeak and wail for two hours is the grand finale of our date."

He froze mid-step at his slip of the tongue. Now he'd gone and done it—and possibly ruined their evening together.

Riley was walking close to Zach's other side, but he appeared lost in his surroundings, taking in the tall buildings and flashing lights.

He knew Delia had heard what he said. She looked as uncomfortable as he felt. His heart and his lungs ceased functioning as he waited for her response.

"I—you," she stammered before she stopped to compose herself. She looked at the ground and then back up at him. "The violins weren't squeaking or wailing. You should get your ears checked."

His breath left his lungs in an audible whoosh as relief flooded through him. He didn't know whether she was accepting this event as a date, but at least she hadn't called it off entirely.

"If you say so," he agreed. "But now comes the real fun."

"Where are we going?"

"Just to the next corner. The symphony is holding a New Year's Eve bash for the VIP ticket holders, which we happen to be. Hence the tuxes." He flashed her a toothy grin.

By that time they had arrived at the hotel and were swept up into a large group of guests that were likewise visiting the party. Zach grabbed Riley's hand and Delia's arm so they wouldn't get separated.

After visiting the coatroom, Zach found them places to sit at a table near the dance floor. There were already several couples whirling about the room in time to— *thankfully*—country music.

This was Texas after all. Formal wear or not, there were some things a Texan just didn't change—like the boots he was wearing in lieu of dress shoes.

"I'd better try to get us our drinks," Zach suggested after he'd seated Delia and Riley. "It's not too long until midnight, and we'll want to toast in the New Year, right?"

"Do I get to toast, too?" Riley asked excitedly.

Zach nodded and ruffled his hair, which was out of place anyway. "You, too, champ. I think I see some fruit punch at the serving table over there. Sound good? Delia?"

"Yes, please," she replied. "That sounds delicious. I'm parched."

Riley just nodded. His attention was already on what was happening in the ballroom. His tie had become unhooked somewhere during the walk over to the hotel, but Zach didn't try to refasten it. If it weren't for Delia, Zach himself would have slipped his tie off a long time ago—or else he would never have worn one at all.

He chuckled when a waiter approached Riley and offered him a festive hat, a horn and some confetti for the big moment. The boy's mouth formed the same wide round *O* as his eyes, which were glittering with excitement.

Zach assumed it would take him only a minute to get the drinks, but the line was long and it seemed like it took him forever to reach the front. He was almost as anxious and fidgety as Riley.

He didn't want to be away from his family for even a moment, much less a quarter of an hour. He was relieved that he hadn't actually *missed* the midnight countdown by the time he returned to the table with three stemware glasses of punch.

"Remember to save some for the toast," Zach reminded Riley as he handed the boy a flute and took a sip of his own drink.

"Nice hats," he commented wryly as he slid into a chair next to Delia and let his free arm drop around the back of her chair. She'd selected a fake-jeweled tiara, which he thought was fitting for the woman he'd always privately thought of as *princess*. He winked at Riley, who had his pointed cap tilted off to one side of his head.

"I didn't get you one," Delia said, laughing through a counterfeit frown. "You can probably hunt a waiter down if you're interested."

She and Riley looked at him in expectation, but he shook his head fiercely. He would do a lot of things for Delia and his son, but there was no way he was going to wear one of those silly hats.

Luckily, they had no time to protest. The countdown to the New Year had suddenly started.

Ten. Nine. Eight.

Seven. Six.

He handed Delia her glass and reached for his own. She thanked him softly, her breath warm against his cheek.

Five. Four. Three.

The three of them watched the big timer on the wall as they enthusiastically shouted the countdown along with the rest of the partygoers.

Zach's pulse raced toward the finish line. For maybe the first time in his life, he was truly looking forward to the New Year.

Two.

They lifted their glasses. Delia shifted toward him and that sweet coconut scent of her shampoo sent his head spinning.

One.

Riley jumped the gun and started clinking his glass with theirs.

Thank you, Lord, for the gift of family.

"Happy New Year!" the three of them chorused together. The same sentiment echoed all around them as the room filled with cheerful cries.

"Happy New Year, honey," Delia said softly, pressing a kiss to Riley's forehead despite his protests. "I think this is going to be a good one."

"Happy New Year, champ," Zach added, once again ruffling his son's hair.

"Happy New Year back," Riley announced proudly. "To both of you guys."

There was a pregnant pause as Riley crossed his arms and stared, first at Delia and then at Zach. The boy's eyebrows rose and disappeared under the black lock of hair that had fallen over his forehead.

"Hello-o-o?" Riley said, drawing out the word in the form of a question.

"What?" Zach's heart reached his throat and lodged there with an anticipation he couldn't yet name.

Riley scoffed and shook his head. He rolled his eyes at Delia.

"It's New Year's, Mom," he said, as if that explained everything.

Delia nodded but looked confused. "And?"

Zach had been too distracted by his own thoughts to realize exactly where Riley was going with this, but suddenly he understood. His skin prickled and all his senses went into overdrive. He was keenly aware of Delia beside him, of every tiny move she made, of the way she instinctively shifted toward him, whether she yet realized Riley's intent.

"And you two guys are supposed to kiss."

Leave it to a kid to tell it like it was—or at least how it was supposed to be.

"Dad?" Riley prompted.

Delia stiffened but didn't move out of his grasp. She shook her head as if she were about to argue, but really what was the point?

It was New Year's and traditions were traditions after all.

And Riley had called him *Dad*.

Even though he'd only known about Riley for a little over a week, Zach had been waiting his whole life for those words. And he realized with a sudden burst of insight that he'd been waiting for ten years to do exactly what Riley had suggested.

Zach turned toward Delia, leaving one hand on her

waist and brushing the fingers of his other hand across the softness of her cheek and into her thick, silky hair.

It had been too long since he'd held her in his arms. He wasn't about to miss the opportunity he'd been presented.

Besides, Riley was watching, waiting for his mother and his father to connect in a real, tangible way. How could he disappoint his son?

Zach's breath quivered as his gaze met Delia's. He could feel the tension in her back and see the hesitancy in her eyes. She was reluctant and unsure of herself—of them.

And yet, for all that, there was something more in her gaze, something drawing him in, although he couldn't put a name to it.

Yearning? Acceptance?

Hope?

His gaze dropped, centering on her full, bow-shaped lips. Her breath was warm as it swept over his chin. He imagined he could almost hear the rapid beating of her heart.

She wasn't protesting. She wasn't moving away.

Maybe it was all for Riley's sake, but at this moment, he would take what he could get. Whether it led anywhere from here was anyone's guess, but he wasn't as averse to the idea as he'd once been.

Drawing out the moment to savor every second of it, he lowered his head and brushed his lips against hers.

Chapter Seventeen

Riley cheered and clapped his hands. His applause jerked Delia back to the present like the crack of a whip. She'd been somewhere else, in another time and another place. She and Zach might have a history together, but this kiss felt new. Different. Exciting.

And she wanted more.

More that she couldn't have. As much as she might want it, she and Zach could not go back in time. She couldn't repair the damage she'd done to him, and he would never forgive her—not that she blamed him.

If only she could have a do-over.

But second chances weren't reality. And idle trips down memory lane would do her no good.

She put her palm against Zach's chest and pushed away, but not before her fingers felt the pounding of his racing heart. His brown eyes were filled with warmth and affection, and she had to turn her gaze away. His feelings were no doubt the temporary effect of their embrace. She couldn't count on them to be real.

Riley had no idea what he had asked when he had brought them together. To him it was simple, in the way only a child could look at it. Two adults—one male, one female—following tradition.

Bringing in the New Year with a kiss.

Oh, no, she thought as she quickly gathered her purse to leave. The tickle of the pulse in her temple exploded to a sharp burst of adrenaline through her head.

For Riley, it wasn't merely one male, one female.

It was Mom and Dad.

Her epiphany was as clear as a sunny Texas morning. Only she'd come about the realization too late.

If she'd guessed what was going through Riley's head, she would never have allowed Zach to kiss her. But she'd been so caught up in the moment, her heart and her mind so in tune with him, that she hadn't realized that Riley had had ulterior motives.

And now he would be hurt.

She sighed deeply. Once again, it was her fault.

She was quiet as they returned to the truck and began the long drive back to Serendipity. Zach appeared lost in his thoughts. He kept his eyes on the road and never so much as glanced at Delia, although occasionally the corner of his mouth tipped up in a thoughtful half smile.

Under normal circumstances she would have been worried about what he might be thinking, but at the moment, it was all she could do to regroup her own emotions.

Turning halfway in her seat, she covered a sleeping Riley with Zach's jacket. He'd curled up around the seat belt with his chin tucked to his shoulder and a soft smile on his face. He'd certainly had a full day—one that he'd never forget, thanks to Zach.

Neither would she, for that matter.

Which brought her back to the kiss.

"We need to talk about what happened," she said, using every ounce of her determination to steady her voice. She took a deep breath and tried to ignore the incessant throbbing that had appeared behind her left eye.

"Tonight was special, and I think—" Zach said at the same time.

"Go ahead," she offered, guessing he was on the same wavelength she was. It was best just to get this out in the open, and if he wanted to be the one to say the words, so much the better.

"No, you," Zach countered politely.

She shook her head, but he insisted.

"Ladies first."

She took a deep breath and spoke as she exhaled, her words in one long string as if they were all attached together. "I think we gave Riley the wrong impression tonight."

The truck jerked a little to the side as he wrenched the wheel, but he quickly recovered.

"How is that?" His voice was low and he sounded genuinely perplexed.

Hadn't he realized what a quandary they were in? She pressed her fingers to her forehead and prayed for the right words and the courage to continue.

"You know he was pushing us to kiss each other."

"Well, sure. I thought it was kind of cute."

Delia chuckled despite her stress. "It was kind of cute. It was also kind of foolish on our part."

Furtively, she glanced at him. Zach shook his head but kept his eyes on the road. A muscle twitched in his jaw but he did not speak.

"I think he believes we are getting back together."

There.

She'd said it.

"And you want to make sure that he knows we are not a couple." Zach's usually honey-rich tenor voice sounded deep and gravelly and emphasized his accent.

"Exactly. When we kissed each other, we put false ideas into his head. Now he's going to start thinking we're a real family."

Zach scoffed. "We can't have that."

Delia's eyes widened and she pressed her lips together to hold back a sob. "No, we can't."

"What do you propose we do about it?" Zach asked after a long pause. "Do you want to talk to him, or do you want me to do it?"

She shook her head. "I think it would be better if we just let this one slide—wait and see how things go. Maybe—I mean, I hope—I'm wrong about this. We just need to be extra careful around one another so he doesn't get the wrong impression. If he starts pushing us together, then we'll have to speak to him about it."

"Okay."

That was his only response. And to her surprise, Delia realized that was not the answer she'd been looking for.

Her heart was breaking, but it wasn't so much of a snapping sensation as it was crushing, like something far more painful than the migraine behind her eye. She didn't know if she could bear it.

But she had to do what needed to be done, and then she needed to stand strong and secure in the decisions she'd made. There was never any doubt that she'd always put Riley's needs ahead of her own, no matter what the consequences to her own heart might be.

She forced herself to reiterate the terms in her mind. She and Zach were not a couple. They were parents who needed to work out an acceptable custody arrangement for their son.

Only that wasn't what she really wanted.

It was time she faced the truth—the *whole* truth. She still cared for Zach—very much.

And if she was being honest with herself, that wasn't exactly new information. It was also not anything she would ever act upon—*could* ever act upon.

By his words, Zach had made his feelings crystal clear. There was no chance whatsoever of reconciliation. It was important that Riley not think otherwise. The last thing she wanted to do was to give her son false hope about something that would never be.

She'd been the one who'd pointed out their dilemma in the first place. She'd been the one to bring up the topic in conversation.

So how could she possibly have been hurt by the conclusions they'd arrived at? She'd become the epitome of a country ballad—an utter fool.

It was all Zach could do to keep the truck on the road. He clenched the wheel tightly with both hands to relieve some of his anxiety, but it wasn't enough. Tension built in the back of his shoulders and fanned into his neck and his jaw.

He'd thought something had changed the moment his lips had met Delia's, but obviously he'd been mistaken. She clearly still believed he hadn't changed—or maybe he was too much a reminder of all she'd gone through alone.

He should have told her how much he still cared for her when he'd had her in his arms.

Now he'd lost his chance.

Or maybe he'd never had a chance at all.

He'd always known Delia was a strong, independent woman, but he was only now realizing just how much. She was not only all right surviving on her own as a single mother, but she thrived on it. How many people could say they made it through college, through *med* school as a single parent?

She was one tough cookie. She didn't need him in her life. She didn't even think she needed God's help.

And in that, at least, she was wrong.

With all his might, Zach rounded up the hurricane of his emotions and pressed them deep into his heart. He had been praying for Delia, that he could forgive her and that they could learn to coexist.

Maybe this was a start.

He couldn't close his eyes because he was driving, but even so he refocused his mind and heart on God.

He didn't know how much time passed, but suddenly he realized just how quiet the cab of the truck had become. The acute, intense silence loomed over him until he couldn't stand it anymore.

"So what did you think of the church service the other day?" he asked, hoping the change in subject wouldn't be too abrupt for her and anticipating that she would welcome the opportunity to speak about *anything* else.

After leaning back to check on Riley, she folded her hands in her lap and sighed. "It was overwhelming."

"I guess the situation wasn't exactly normal, was it, with everyone wanting to know about Riley? The townsfolk are wonderful, but they can be a little overpowering when they get curious, especially as many of our neighbors were attending church that day."

"There is that," Delia agreed with a chuckle that Zach thought sounded a little forced. "But that was the whole point of going, right—to introduce Riley as your son?"

She paused and brushed at an invisible wrinkle in her dress. "It wasn't the neighbors overwhelming me. At least, that's not what I meant."

"No?"

"No." She sighed softly. "I wasn't sure how I was going to feel about going back to church again. I haven't stepped foot in a church since I left Serendipity."

"Really? Not even once?"

She shook her head. "Not even once. At first it was because I was adjusting to living in a big city. The churches were large and a bit daunting in and of themselves, never mind how many people attended services there. I decided to settle in a bit before I started looking for a church."

"And then?"

"And then I found out I was pregnant."

Zach's shoulders tightened as he imagined how it had been for Delia, all alone in a large city completely across the coast from her hometown, only to find out she was carrying a child.

"So you had no church family to support you."

"No." Her jaw rocked forward. "And I decided I didn't care. I set aside my faith. I became a self-made woman."

Zach paused, brushing his thumb along the ridge of his jaw. "I am in awe of you, I really am," he said sincerely. "You are the strongest, most compelling woman I've ever met. But I don't believe your independence and your faith have to be mutually exclusive. Do you?"

"That's just it. I realized when I came back here that there is no such thing as true independence. I wasn't self-made, I was God-made, whether I chose to acknowledge His presence and His work in my life or not."

"Unless the Lord builds the house, the workers labor in vain, right? So you're not angry with me for taking you to church?"

He could feel Delia's gaze on him, but he didn't look away from the road. He was happy to hear of God's grace working in Delia's life. His eyes were burning, but he was a guy—he didn't cry, and he didn't want Delia to see just how close he was to tears.

However confused Zach was about everything else, Delia renewing her faith *was* a direct answer to prayer, and he was more thankful than he could put into words.

"I'm not mad," she said, turning her head so she was looking out the passenger-side window. Her voice so soft Zach could barely hear her. "I'm grateful."

She paused and brushed her hair away from her face with her palm. "I have to tell you, I'm so glad God brought you into Riley's life. You're going to make all the difference in the world to that little boy."

That was all she was asking of him, and he'd certainly step up to the plate where Riley was concerned. Being a dad meant everything to him.

But now he was beginning to think he wanted more.

Chapter Eighteen

Delia's personal life might have been in shambles, but the town clinic was enormously successful. She'd been putting in full five-day weeks and on-call weekends now that her friends and neighbors knew she was open for business. Most of her cases were fairly insignificant, issues that people had put off getting checked on because they didn't care to drive an hour to see a doctor.

Coughs. Colds. Strains. Sprains.

No real emergencies to speak of, but then, she hadn't expected any. Not much went on in a quiet town like Serendipity, nothing that Delia found difficult to handle on her own. No drug overdoses. No children coming in with bloody, sometimes-fatal gunshot wounds from drive-by gang shootings.

To her surprise, she found she didn't miss the fast-paced, high-adrenaline discord of a Baltimore emergency room as much as she'd thought she might. Small-town life was definitely beginning to agree with her.

Delia glanced at her watch. Seven-thirty. She'd been supposed to get off at six, but today the waiting room had been extra full—not that she minded. Keeping herself physically and mentally occupied at the tiny clinic was just what the doctor ordered.

Anything to keep herself from thinking about Zach.

She grabbed an empty cloth sack and began stuffing dirty linens inside, which she intended to wash in her mother's machine at home later that evening. She didn't mind the extra work, and Riley liked to help her fold.

It was her favorite moment of the day, sharing special one-on-one time with her son. He'd talk about his day, and she'd tell him about hers. Sometimes he'd talk about Zach, which Delia found painful, but it was for the best. She had to learn to deal with it sometime. Riley was so enthused about his dad, his friends and his new life in Serendipity that she could not help but share his joy. She certainly didn't want to put a damper on his feelings. She'd never seen him happier.

But for Delia, evenings were tougher than the days. When she closed her eyes to sleep, all she saw was Zach.

Not that she'd actually physically *seen* Zach in the two weeks that had gone by since the symphony. The truth was, she'd flat-out *avoided* him, going out of her way to be absent whenever he visited her parents' house to spend time with Riley.

She was a coward. Guilt hovered over her like a black cloud. She couldn't steer clear of Zach forever. It was this kind of attitude that had gotten her into trouble in the first place. Hadn't she learned her lesson from her past mistakes? The longer she waited, the harder it would be.

It wasn't likely to be a confrontation anyway. They'd

said everything that needed to be said in the truck on New Year's Eve.

With a scoff, she reached into the basket for what was left of the linens and then tied the bag up tight.

She resolved then and there to move forward in her life. What frightened her was her own heart. Now that she knew for certain how she felt about Zach, she wasn't sure she'd be able to hide it from him.

He'd always been able to read her like a book. How would he react if he knew the real truth? She'd persistently shoved her feelings behind closed doors and had turned the key in the lock, but she was still afraid that it would take no more than a moment with Zach to make the doors burst open again.

That's why she'd been dragging her feet, hoping that if she gave herself a little time she'd be more in control of her emotions. Unfortunately, that hadn't happened.

And it probably wouldn't.

She picked up the laundry bag and groaned. It was heavier than she'd expected. Her emotions felt the same way—an enormous, awkward burden to carry, much weightier than she possibly could have imagined when she moved back to Serendipity.

She hadn't realized she'd still have such deep feelings for Zach. But she was strong. She'd get over it.

She would.

Shifting the bag to one side, she reached for the keys in her jacket pocket. Most people in Serendipity didn't bother locking their doors, but Delia made an exception for the clinic because the pharmacy, such as it was, was located inside.

She'd just turned the key in the lock when the telephone rang. For a split second she considered ignoring it. It was already an hour and a half past normal clinic hours and she was exhausted. Vicki, her receptionist, had left hours ago.

Surely the caller could wait until tomorrow. And if it was a true emergency, they could always call 9-1-1.

But compassion immediately trumped fatigue, as it always did with Delia. This was Serendipity after all. She likely knew the caller. And even if she didn't, she was the town's only physician. The least she could do was answer the telephone and find out what the problem was—if there was one. More than likely she'd simply be able to schedule the caller for an appointment in the morning. How much of a hassle could that be?

Having made her decision, she reentered the clinic and dropped the laundry bag just inside the door, racing to reach the telephone before the caller hung up or the call was transferred to voice mail.

"Hello?" she asked on the seventh ring, just barely avoiding the voice mail.

"Yes, ma'am," a deep, scratchy voice returned. "May I speak to Delia, please? It's an emergency."

She recognized his voice immediately. Chance Hawkins had been in a serious car accident years before, which had affected his ability to speak, leaving him sounding low and raspy.

"Speaking," Delia replied. "Is this Chance? Is everything okay? You sound worried."

"I'm calling about Phoebe," he said, his voice even more strained than usual. "She's in labor."

"Okay." Delia eased herself into a chair and lifted her legs, crossing her ankles on the cold, flat surface of the desk. Her feet were aching and it felt good to put them up for a moment. "Do you have a birthing plan? How far apart are the contractions?"

She kept her voice calm and controlled. She wasn't concerned. In her experience, men had the tendency to panic when their wives went into labor, usually with no good cause other than that they had absolutely no control over the situation.

"We were supposed to go to Mercy Medical Center in San Antonio, only now I'm not sure Phoebe's going to make it. She's in a lot of pain."

Delia smiled indulgently because no one could see it. They didn't call it labor for nothing. The intensity of the pain caught even the most prepared of couples off guard, both mom and dad alike. This was Phoebe's first pregnancy, which generally meant hours of labor. Surely they had plenty of time to get to a hospital before the real fun began.

"How far apart are her contractions?" she asked again because Chance appeared to be distracted and hadn't answered her question.

"I've been timing them with a stopwatch," he assured her. "When they first started they were twelve minutes apart. The doctor told us to head for the hospital when they reached ten-minute intervals because we have so far to travel."

He took a deep, raspy breath. "We were just about to walk out the door when suddenly Phoebe screamed in pain and crumpled to the floor. I don't know what happened, but now the contractions are coming one right after the other. She barely has time to catch a breath between them. Aunt Jo took Lucy to a friend's house a couple of towns over, so she's not here to help, and I don't know what I should do. Call an ambulance?"

Halfway through Chance's explanation, Delia scrambled from her seat and started gathering supplies. She had an emergency medical bag already prepared and stored in the trunk of her car, but that was for general emergencies like cuts and sprains—certainly not childbirth.

She prayed as she went. Talking to God was becoming more natural now—almost as effortless as it had been when she was a teenager. *Dear Lord, reassure Phoebe and Chance with Your presence and Your peace.*

"Where is Phoebe now?" she asked as she exited the clinic and locked the door for the second time that evening.

"I put her on our bed," he replied, sounding as if he was the one in agony. "I don't think I can move her again. It will hurt her too much."

"Don't try to move her," Delia instructed. "Just stay with her and do your best to keep her calm. If you have a moment between her contractions, find her some extra pillows to get her as comfortable as possible and maybe offer her some ice chips." She thought it might help to give Chance something productive to do while he waited for her arrival.

Chance didn't answer immediately. Delia could hear Phoebe moaning in the background, and Chance was talking her through the contraction.

"Just remember," Delia cautioned him when Phoebe's contraction was over and Chance's attention was once more on her. "The most important thing for you to do right now is just to stay by her side and reassure her that everything is going to be all right."

"*Is* everything going to be all right?"

"Of course," she said in an encouraging tone. "Women have babies every day. Your little one is just overly anxious to make his or her debut."

"So you don't think I should call an ambulance?"

"From what you've told me, I don't think they would be able to get her to the hospital fast enough. You just take care of that wife of yours. I'll call the paramedics for backup, but I don't want you to worry. I've delivered plenty of babies on my ob/gyn rotation, so I'm experienced with childbirth. Just hang in there for a few more minutes, okay?"

Delia was already halfway to the Hawkins home as she spoke. Fortunately, the clinic wasn't far from most of the homesteads, and the Hawkins lived just outside of town.

"I'm going to hang up now, Chance," she informed him. "I have a couple of calls to make before I get to your house."

Chance assented, but he didn't sound too sure of himself.

Delia immediately speed-dialed her parents' house to let her mother know she was going to be late, and to go ahead and feed Riley and tuck him in bed for the night without her.

After she hung up with her mom, she clutched her cell phone to her chest and sighed. This was going to be difficult, but there was no time to be wishy-washy.

She had no doubt she could deliver Phoebe's baby safely, but she knew Chance would be less than useless if she needed assistance, and he'd indicated that Jo wasn't there to help.

She needed to call a medic, just to be on the safe

side. Besides, they'd need to transport Phoebe and her baby to the hospital after the birth for a checkup.

She needed Zach.

She knew as she dialed the number to the fire department that no one else would do. Zach wouldn't just lend her assistance, he would lend her strength and encouragement. She was confident in her skills and abilities as a doctor, but she'd been in medicine long enough to know that things often didn't go exactly as anticipated. Better to be safe than sorry.

Ben Atwood answered the telephone at the fire department.

"Ben, this is Delia Ivers," she stated, skipping formalities. "Is Zach around?"

"He's out right now, but he'll be back soon. He just went out to grab some spaghetti from his house. We have a bottle of pasta sauce here but not the noodles, and the men are all starving."

Delia forced a laugh.

"You sound a little tense. Is everything all right?"

"Everything is fine," she assured him. "There's a bit of an emergency at the Hawkins residence. Phoebe's gone into labor and it sounds like I may be delivering her right there at the house. I shouldn't have any trouble delivering the baby, but I'll need an ambulance to transport Phoebe and the little one to the hospital afterward."

"And you want Zach to assist with the birth." It wasn't a question, and Ben didn't wait for an answer before continuing. "I'll leave right now and pick Zach up on the way. He'll be there as soon as I can get him there."

Ben hadn't said *we'll* be there soon, even though

he'd be the second paramedic in the ambulance. She had a feeling Ben understood what she couldn't put into words.

"Thanks, Ben. I'll see you."

Delia hung up the phone just as she pulled into the Hawkinses' driveway. She grabbed the bag she'd packed for the delivery and then stopped to get her regular medical bag from the trunk. By the time she got to the front porch, Chance had the door open and was waiting for her.

"Point me the way to Phoebe," she said without preamble.

Chance nearly ran across the family room and down the hallway, stopping at the door to a large master bedroom.

"Phoebe, honey, Delia is here to help with the baby," he said gently.

As Delia followed Chance down the hallway, she was already mentally reviewing the supplies she'd be needing for the delivery, so she was unprepared for Phoebe's response to Chance's announcement.

A shrill, spine-tingling scream.

Chapter Nineteen

Zach had finally found the box of spaghetti he'd known was somewhere in his pathetic excuse for a pantry. He hadn't realized it was such a mess until he was looking for something specific. Usually he just pushed items around until he found whatever suited his appetite at the moment.

He had just tucked the box under his arm and switched off the kitchen light when he heard the ambulance approaching.

Pure adrenaline pumped through him in what had become a natural physical reaction to the peal of sirens. He'd been a paramedic long enough to associate the sound with action.

Surprisingly—or maybe not so much—his first thought was of Delia and Riley. They lived just up the road a ways. Had they been hurt?

The fact that there were half a dozen other ranch houses between his house and Delia's didn't even occur to him. He dropped the box of spaghetti on the table and raced toward the front door, hoping to see which way the ambulance was headed.

He was supposed to be at the station, so he knew they would be shorthanded without him. Ben would need him to follow. He already had the keys to his truck in his hand. He'd have to hurry if he wanted to catch up.

To Zach's astonishment, Ben pulled the ambulance straight into his driveway. The reflection of flashing red-and-blue lights glared off the front windows of his house. His grinning partner flipped the siren switch off and then on again as he rolled down his window.

"I got tired of waiting for you to get back with the food," Ben teased.

"Turn that thing off," Zach said as he climbed into the passenger seat. "Or is there a real emergency I don't know about?"

"Not an emergency exactly," Ben explained, turning off the siren and the flashing lights and backing out of Zach's driveway. "Phoebe Hawkins's baby decided to show up unexpectedly."

Zach snorted. "I'd hardly call it unexpected. I saw her at the café the other day and she looked like she was about ready to pop."

"Well, she's popping now," Ben replied with a chuckle. "And apparently the kid won't wait long enough for his mama to get him to the hospital."

"So we're taking Phoebe by ambulance?" Zach asked. "Maybe you should turn that siren back on."

"Delia should already be there," Ben replied. "And she didn't sound overly concerned. But she did think she was going to have to deliver the baby at the house."

"Alone? Step on it, man," Zach exclaimed, fastening his seat belt.

Ben laughed but didn't go any faster than the speed

limit. Zach fidgeted in his seat. He wanted to be with Delia *now*.

"Oh, and by the way," Ben continued with a smirk, "the pretty lady doctor specifically asked for you."

His heart lurched almost painfully into his throat despite the fact that adrenaline already had his pulse working overtime. Even just thinking about Delia made him feel a little bit over the edge, in the way that even the thrill of paramedic work could not. With Delia, he wasn't working to save a life, he was working to save a relationship.

Or at least he would be, when he saw her again, which had not happened since New Year's Eve.

And he knew why.

Their lives had become too complicated. They wouldn't have to deal with *not* being a couple in front of Riley if they were never seen together by him. It made sense, in a Delia kind of way, which was why he was giving her space to figure things out on her own.

And now she was asking for him?

Maybe delivering Phoebe's baby was more complicated than Delia had let on to Ben. He couldn't think of any other likely reason for this sudden turnaround. It couldn't be personal, could it?

Despite trying to temper it down with reason, hope flared like a wildfire in his chest.

The moment Ben pulled into the driveway and put on the brakes, Zach pulled out his paramedic bag and headed toward the Hawkinses' front door, full speed ahead. He didn't knock, nor did he wait for someone to come to the door. Because the house was unlocked, he let himself in, knowing both Chance and Delia would be busy with Phoebe.

"Paramedics," he called loudly as he jogged toward what he hoped was the hallway to the bedrooms.

"Over here," Chance called back.

Knowing he was going the right direction, he increased his speed. His need to be with Delia was burning in his chest, as was the desire to aid Phoebe, fueled by what was now the true course of his life. He'd become a paramedic to help people, in part to make up for all the hurt he'd caused as a youth.

As he entered the room, he found Chance by Phoebe's bedside. She held his hand in a death grip, his fingers turning white from how tightly she was squeezing, but Chance was not complaining. He looked concerned, and anxious and at loose ends.

Zach couldn't imagine watching the woman he loved with his whole heart suffer such torment, even if it was to introduce new life into the world. And yet contrarily he wished he had been there for Delia when she'd delivered Riley, holding her hand like Chance was doing now for Phoebe.

Delia dabbed at Phoebe's forehead with a cold washcloth. "It won't be long now, honey," she encouraged softly. "Just keep your eyes on Chance. He'll help you breathe through your contractions."

Zach approached and laid a hand on Delia's shoulder. "What do you need me to do?"

Her eyes met his, her relief at his presence evident in her smile. "You came."

He didn't know what to say to that. Of course he'd come. Besides the fact that he was a paramedic and it was his job to handle emergencies, he would always be there for her, in every situation, no matter what.

"I'm here," he said, his voice almost as low and raspy as Chance's.

Her gaze turned back to Phoebe. "She's seven centimeters dilated and fully effaced. She went from four to seven since I've been here—about a half an hour. It won't be long now until she's ready to push. We need to set up some kind of pediatric station to assess the baby once it's born."

"I'm on it, princess," Zach assured her. "And Ben is right behind me. We'll have everything ready to go in a jiff."

"And please call and see if you can get a hold of Jo. I'm sure she and Lucy will want to be here as soon as possible," she added as she turned her attention back to Phoebe.

"You've got it." He hesitated just for a moment, observing her compassionate bedside manner, which incorporated both Phoebe and Chance. This was always how he had pictured her, serving people through her God-given gift of medical training.

He'd never imagined that *he* would likewise fill such a role. If someone would have told him when he was a wild-hearted young teenager that he would someday become a paramedic saving people's lives, he would have laughed in their face.

And look at him now.

Working side by side with Delia, helping to bring the miracle of new life into the world.

He could barely swallow, much less breathe, but it wasn't an unpleasant feeling, the billowing cloud of joy and wonder.

Smiling inwardly, Zach returned to the ambulance, where he found Ben preparing the gurney. Together, they pulled it out of the ambulance, although they decided not to bring it into the house because the baby had yet to be born.

"Delia would like us to prepare a makeshift pediatric station for her," Zach told his partner and friend.

"For *her?*" Ben smirked.

Zach snorted and shook his head. "For the baby. You know what I mean."

"Sure I do," Ben replied with a chuckle. "Whatever you say, man."

Zach reentered the house with Ben right behind him, shaking his head as his partner continued to chuckle.

"I think our best bet is to use their bassinet," Zach said, turning his attention to the business at hand. "I saw it in the corner of their bedroom. If we can pull it into the hallway, we can set up an oxygen tank on standby."

"Sounds good," Ben replied.

"You get the bassinet and I'll find some sheets," Zach suggested.

Ben nodded and headed for the bedroom, while Zach began investigating closets, looking for towels and sheets.

"They're in the cupboard in the bathroom." He hadn't heard Delia approach, but now she was close enough for him to inhale the sweet scent of coconuts.

Even though he had no idea how she'd known what he was looking for, he was glad for the assistance, as he'd just opened the door to his fourth closet and instead of finding the items he was searching for, had instead encountered what was clearly the cleaning closet— housing a vacuum, a mop and a broom, and assorted cans and spray bottles.

He turned and their eyes met. Despite the fact that they were both on duty, his pulse experienced the same jolt it always did when he saw her.

"Thank you," he said deeply, not quite able to mask his emotions.

She looked calm. Composed. Under control.

He felt anything but.

She'd pulled her silky black hair up off her face, but a strand had escaped. He was briefly mesmerized by that single lock of hair, distracted by the way it curled across the blushing rose of her cheek. Inhaling sharply, he reached out and swept it back behind her ear with his fingers, his palm brushing across the softness of her skin.

It was only the smallest movement—in reality no more than a few seconds of time.

Their gazes locked. Powerful rivers of emotions rushed back and forth between them.

Delia broke the contact, looking first at the floor and then over her shoulder to the bedroom where Phoebe labored.

"Can you get me a couple of clean sheets while you're at it?" she asked as if nothing had just happened between them.

He cleared his throat.

"Will do," he said, following her lead. He hadn't forgotten that they had work to do—a baby to deliver safely.

Delia returned to Phoebe, and Zach found the cupboard full of clean sheets and towels in the bathroom right where Delia had indicated. Indiscriminately, he scooped up a handful of sheets, and then piled several colorful bath towels on top of them.

Chance and Phoebe would have a lot of linens to replace, he noted absently as he worked. But he supposed they wouldn't mind. Not when they held their baby in their arms.

Children made everything worth it, any sacrifice a pleasure.

Zach returned to the bedroom and placed half the pile of sheets and towels on a nearby chair. Delia was once again busy tending to Phoebe and merely nodded her thanks for his filling her request.

Taking the rest of the linens with him, he returned to the end of the hallway, where he found Ben stationing the bassinet.

He laid the sheets aside as the two of them set up an oxygen tank next to the baby's bed. Zach hoped they wouldn't have to use it, but he knew it was common enough for newborns to need a little extra air when they took their first breath.

Phoebe screamed and a chill sprinted down Zach's spine. He never imagined having a baby could be so heartrending. He didn't know how Chance could bear it, much less Phoebe.

Experiencing the real thing was far from taking an exam on paper. He'd only seen one emergency childbirth in his ride-along field training, and he'd been watching, not participating. The woman had been in a car on her way to the hospital and she hadn't quite made it. Her baby had been born quickly and without much of a fuss. It seemed to Zach that whatever Phoebe was experiencing was quite different—and maybe much worse.

He returned to the room and stood at the end of the bed, smiling his encouragement to Phoebe as she rested between contractions. She looked exhausted beyond belief and the really hard part—pushing—hadn't even started yet.

He cringed along with Chance as the next contraction started. Delia seemed to be the only one in the room unaffected by Phoebe's condition, calmly talking her through the contraction from start to finish.

"I'm done with this," Phoebe announced as the contraction ended. She sounded as if she meant it with all her heart, as if she were going to rise from the bed and walk right out of the room, leaving the pain and agony behind. "I want out."

Delia chuckled. "There's no way out but through, hon. Just think of your precious baby. I know it doesn't seem like it now, but you'll forget all about the pain the moment your child is in your arms."

"Forgive me if I don't believe you." Phoebe groaned loudly and clenched Chance's hand until it was white with pressure. "Here comes another one. Can this just be over already?"

"Soon," Delia promised. "For now, just concentrate on getting through this one contraction."

Phoebe nodded, but then her face creased with the pain of another contraction.

"The pressure is unbelievable," Phoebe said through gritted teeth. "So intense."

"As soon as this contraction is over, I'm going to check you again," Delia stated, pulling on a pair of neoprene gloves. "I have a feeling you're ready to push."

Zach stepped out of the room to give Phoebe a little privacy.

"We're at zero hour," he informed Ben. "I think she's getting ready to push. The little one may be here soon."

Ben grunted. "That could be hours yet. We're ready when the baby is."

"I know this is Phoebe's first baby, but nothing else has been going by the book on this delivery. I wouldn't be surprised if we don't have to wait as long as you think."

Ben shrugged. "I'm on duty either way. And I'm glad to be here to help the Hawkinses."

"Yeah," Zach agreed, leaning his shoulder against the wall and jamming his hands into the pockets of his blue jeans. "Me, too."

And glad to be here helping Delia, he added silently.

He took a deep breath and closed his eyes, praying for the baby's safe delivery and for God to guide Delia's hands.

He was glad for a moment to regroup, but it didn't last.

"Zach," Delia called from the bedroom, her voice strained. "I need you in here—*now.*"

Chapter Twenty

This baby was coming *now*. Delia couldn't believe it.

Zach sprinted into the room, an expectant look on his face. He pulled up short next to Delia at the foot of the bed. Gazing down on Phoebe, his expression altered to an absorbing combination of determination and compassion.

Love welled in Delia's heart, knowing that this man cared so much. He was as prepared as he could be, but Delia still sensed the tiniest bit of uneasiness in the way he shifted from foot to foot and clenched and unclenched his fists.

He was a man of action. He wanted to be doing, not watching, which was, unfortunately for him, the larger part of delivering a baby—unless you happened to be the mother in question, of course. She well remembered her own birthing experience—one that Zach hadn't been a part of.

Was that why there was a hint of apprehension in his eyes? She was certain no one else in the room could see it, but Delia knew—and the moment her eyes met Zach's, he knew that she saw right through him.

His lips quirked into a half smile and his eyebrows rose.

"What can I do?" he asked pointedly, his gaze turning to Phoebe as she gasped for breath.

"Phoebe needs support when she curls up to push," Delia explained to both of the men.

That was all the direction Zach needed. He stepped to Phoebe's side and gripped her hand, using his other arm to support her under her shoulders as she pushed.

Without a word, Chance quickly followed suit.

"I want you to bear down really hard with this next contraction, Phoebe," Delia encouraged. "The baby's head is crowning. I can see a thatch of black hair. Do you know if it's a boy or a girl?"

Phoebe pinched her lips and shook her head.

"We wanted it to be a surprise," Chance inserted when he saw that Phoebe was unable to speak.

Zach whispered some form of encouragement into Phoebe's ear. Chance was mimicking Zach's movements from the other side of the bed, but rather than speaking, he simply brushed her hair off her face, kissed her forehead, and nodded.

Phoebe smiled resolutely and nodded back at her beloved husband, determination replacing trepidation. That was the expression Delia had been looking for. Phoebe was ready to have this baby.

The next contraction started with an intensity that took Phoebe off guard. She screamed as her body racked with pain. Both men looked to Delia with wide, concerned gazes.

Delia had seen this before. At this point, her job consisted not only of delivering Phoebe's baby and making sure mother and baby were both safe and comfortable, but also keeping two very concerned men on their feet and coherent.

With Chance, it wasn't so hard to imagine why he might be feeling a little bit woozy. Many fathers were overwhelmed by the whole encounter of having a baby and the knowledge of suddenly becoming a father. But because this wasn't Chance's first go-round with childbirth, she hoped he'd hold up just fine.

For Zach, who knew?

She hadn't the slightest idea if he'd ever seen a delivery before, although she assumed his paramedic training included emergency childbirth. Even if it didn't, he had to have seen enough blood and guts during regular rounds not to be squeamish about seeing a baby being born—and yet he definitely looked a little green around the gills. How peculiar.

"Okay, Phoebe, make it a good one," Delia said, reaching for the bulb syringe on the accent table where all her equipment was prepared and waiting.

Phoebe gasped for air and then rolled up, supported by the two men at her sides. She groaned and squeezed their hands tightly and then pushed for all she was worth.

With that effort, the baby's head was visible and Delia quickly cleared the airways of any remaining moisture. What a cute little nose and mouth the infant had. What a blessing.

"Hold on there for a second and just breathe," Delia instructed as she worked. "I know it's hard *not* to push, but please give me just a moment and then we're good to go."

Phoebe panted her way through the rest of the contraction. Zach and Chance both puffed along with her.

They were coaching her, but it struck Delia as humorous to watch the two men gasping for breath as if they were the ones doing the labor.

"This is the last push," Delia said. "Give it all you've got, Phoebe."

Delia supported the baby's head and prepared to turn it so the shoulders could slip through. It was usually a seamless process, and Delia had made dozens of deliveries without incident.

It only took her a second for her to realize something was wrong. The baby wasn't turning. She pulled gently but with no success. The shoulders were firmly wedged and the baby wasn't budging.

They needed to get the baby out *immediately*.

Zach was by her side before she even had the opportunity to ask for his assistance. Somehow he knew there was trouble, even though she hadn't said a word. It was critical for her to stay controlled and keep Phoebe and Chance from panicking.

"The shoulder is lodged in tight," she told him softly. "I don't have any high-tech devices here, so we're going to have to get this baby out the old midwives' way."

"Just tell me what you need me to do." His voice was calm and reassuring, just what she needed to keep her own emotions under control.

She wasn't used to being this emotionally involved in her medical work, but she'd gone to school with Chance, and from the times she'd seen Phoebe socially, she'd gathered that the woman was super-sweet and the perfect woman for him.

Doctors were supposed to remain detached, and for good reason. If anything happened to this baby, she didn't know what she would do. She was responsible for making sure this little life came into the world safely.

She'd faced her own fears, the apprehension of every expecting mother, the day Riley was born. Despite her years in medicine, she couldn't fight the lightning-hot bolts of panic surging through her.

I am with you always.

It wasn't audible speech. Rather those words were heard by her heart and felt in her soul. This baby was God's creation. He knew the days of the child's life before the little one was even born.

Thank you, Lord, for Your presence here, she prayed silently. *Please help us deliver this child safely.*

Zach placed a hand on her shoulder. Their eyes met, his gaze strong and sure.

Zach had faith in God. And he had faith in her.

"We need to push this little one out," she explained, still keeping her voice low. "Phoebe is too weak to do it on her own. Slide your fingers under the shoulder and apply gentle pressure. We have to get this baby turned around."

Zach nodded. Together they worked on the delivery, Phoebe supporting the baby's head and neck while Zach worked on the shoulders.

There was a tense moment when nothing seemed to be happening, and then just as suddenly, the baby was free, sliding out into Delia and Zach's hands with unexpected ease.

The baby scrunched up his little red face and howled.

Zach's fingers touched Delia's. Together, they cradled the precious, perfectly formed bawling infant. Their gazes locked. She'd never before seen the look that was flooding through Zach's eyes, the pure elation of hearing a baby cry for the first time.

She had taken that away from him. He should have experienced the joy of the birth of his own son.

"It's a boy," Zach announced with a laugh as he slid the baby more firmly into Delia's arms so she could transfer him to a wide-eyed Phoebe, who was crying almost as loudly as the baby.

"A boy," Chance repeated, leaning over his wife and newborn son. "Hello, little Aaron."

Phoebe hiccupped. "Aaron Joseph Hawkins. We keep the name in the family, you know. It's traditional."

"Congratulations, you two," Delia said with all her heart. "He's a beautiful boy."

"Handsome," Zach amended. "Boys don't like being called beautiful. Just listen to him protesting."

He was, until the new mama whispered to him.

"Thank you, Jesus," Phoebe said softly, cuddling the infant to her neck and kissing his little cheek. The baby immediately quieted, his dark, cloudy blue eyes staring adoringly at his mother and his little hands reaching up to touch her face.

Delia stepped back, letting the new little family rejoice by themselves for a moment. The bonding time between mother and baby was a sacred thing, especially with the father hovering protectively over both of them.

Full of emotion and wanting to cry herself, she didn't realize Zach had moved to her side until he laid a hand on her shoulder.

"You did a great job," he said, leaning close to her ear. "You should be proud of yourself."

"I never would have made it without you."

Now she was *really* about to cry. A tumult of emotion built from deep within her, all the many things she'd kept hidden all these years suddenly threatening to explode. She closed her eyes as she struggled to keep her feelings contained thinking her chest might burst from the effort.

All this time, she'd gone it alone. Zach hadn't been there to see the birth of *his* son, and it was all her fault. She had denied him one of the most precious moments in a man's life. He had to realize that now.

And he had to hate her for it.

As if he'd read her mind, he dropped his hand from her arm and moved to the bedside.

"Ben and I need to check this little guy over real quick," he said to Phoebe, who gave Aaron one last cuddle before reluctantly handing him over to Zach.

Zach didn't immediately head for the hallway. He stood immobile, cradling the new life in his arms, staring at the child with such an expression of wonder that Delia felt as if she'd suddenly been pierced by a million jagged fragments of glass.

What a horrible, *horrible* thing she'd done.

Zach carried the infant into the hallway where Ben was waiting. Delia still had work to do, so she returned to Phoebe, using the familiarity of practicing medicine to distance herself from the barrage of emotions she would eventually have to deal with.

And she *would* have to deal with them. She only hoped that she'd be able to hold them in until Zach was gone.

Chapter Twenty-One

Something was bothering Delia, and Zach couldn't imagine what it could be. She'd just taken part in an amazing birth experience. Aaron was a perfectly formed, strong-lunged baby boy who hadn't even needed any oxygen.

She should be thrilled at how well this home birth had progressed—and she should be proud of herself for a job well done, not to mention full of joy at introducing a new life into God's world.

But she wasn't any of those things. Now that Jo and Lucy had arrived, Delia remained in the background, her arms wrapped tightly around her middle. If Zach didn't miss his guess, she was on the verge of tears.

Happy tears?

He didn't think so.

"Thank You, Jesus, thank You Lord," Jo exclaimed as she scooped little Aaron into her arms. "Look at that cute little button of a nose. And Chance, dear, I think he's going to have your dark eyes. He's definitely got your hair.

"But you favor your mama in good looks, now, don't

you, sweetie? You're a real little beauty," she cooed to Aaron.

The baby squealed.

Zach stepped closer to Delia. He was near enough to be invading her personal space, but she didn't appear to notice he was there.

"Listen to little Aaron protesting," he observed with a chuckle.

Delia's gaze shot to him and she blinked as if coming out of a fog.

"The baby," Zach clarified. "Why does everyone keep calling him beautiful? Anyone with ears can tell he has an issue with it."

Delia's lips screwed up in that cute little expression she had when she was thinking about something. "It seems to me that *you're* the one with the problem."

Zach snorted. "I'm not insecure. I just know I wouldn't want anyone to consider me beautiful, much less say it out loud."

She looked at him for a long moment before speaking.

"You *are* beautiful," she said in a low, rich tone that wavered a little bit as she spoke. Her gaze met his momentarily, but then she quickly looked away.

He tried to swallow and couldn't. His heart was so full of yearning that he wanted to wrap her in his arms right now and kiss her senseless—just to show her how much of a man he was.

But given the circumstances, and Delia's current opinion of their relationship, that would have been the worst thing hc could do. So with effort, he restrained himself, although he doubted anyone elsc in the room would have noticed, as intent as they all were to the new addition to the world.

"Well, now," he conceded, lengthening his drawl as he pretended to consider her words. "It doesn't sound quite so bad coming from you."

Color rose on her face, but she smiled. His heart clenched.

He loved Delia, and if it took his whole life, he would prove he was the man she needed him to be. He hoped that when they were sharing a porch swing in the twilight of their lives, he might still be able to say something to make shades of attractive color splash across her cheeks.

She'd been genuinely pleased by what he said—or at least, he'd thought she'd been. It was a start. And then a moment later the smile dropped from her lips and she turned away. But before she did, he saw the expression on her face and the look in her eye.

She was confused, maybe even disturbed about something.

What had flashed through her mind? Why the sudden change in demeanor?

He reached for her shoulder, intending to turn her around and ask her, but she shrugged him off and darted forward and back into the stream of the family's celebration.

Zach stayed next to the door, his gaze never leaving her. He would never understand the hot-and-cold nature of women, and Delia in particular, if he lived to be a hundred.

"What do you think of your new baby brother, Lucy?" Delia asked, with what Zach thought was a rather forced grin.

The girl, who was sitting on the edge of the bed on Chance's side, shrugged detachedly, but Zach could see that her eyes were alight with interest. He suspected Delia could see that as well, if her next actions were anything to go by.

She scooped the baby from Jo's arms and held him to Lucy, who immediately sprang from the bed and stepped backward, tucking her hands into the back pockets of her blue-jean overalls.

Delia didn't push her. Rather, she turned so Lucy could see the baby's face better.

"I think he looks like you."

Lucy chuckled hesitantly and reached toward Aaron. The baby promptly clamped his little fist onto her finger and thrust it into his mouth.

"Oh," she exclaimed.

"See?" Delia encouraged. "He likes you already."

"Well, of course he likes her," Jo agreed fervently. "He's her baby brother. He knows which person in this room will give him the real scoop on things."

Aaron gurgled as if in agreement and everyone laughed.

"I think I'm going to cry," Phoebe said with a hiccup.

Chance smiled. "Darlin', you've been bawling since the moment this kid was born."

Phoebe wrinkled her nose and stuck her tongue out at Chance. "You know I can't help it. I always cry when I'm happy."

Chance leaned down and kissed his wife affectionately on the forehead. "Then I'm glad to hear you crying, love."

Zach's heart lodged itself squarely in his throat. He

tried to swallow, but that didn't work, so he coughed instead.

The only one who seemed to notice was Delia, who turned toward him with her dark eyebrows arched.

"Are you okay?" she queried.

"I—yeah," Zach said and then hacked some more.

He couldn't even look her in the eye without wanting to scoop her up into his arms and run for the altar. Never mind that the church was a couple of miles away and that the preacher was no doubt home asleep with his wife.

Did she see how flustered she made him? If she did, she didn't give him any hint of it. Or maybe she just didn't care.

"Ben went out front to get the gurney," he said in a raspy voice. "We need to get Phoebe and Aaron transported to Mercy so they can both be checked out."

"Of course." Her gaze flickered with emotion, but Zach couldn't begin to guess what it was. He'd lost his equilibrium a long time ago, and his own feelings were flaying about like the end of a whip.

Delia looked like she might want to say more, but after a moment, she simply pinched her lips and turned back to the happy scene.

"Time to get mama and baby bundled up and ready to go down to the hospital," she announced.

Delia swaddled Aaron in an extra receiving blanket and held the baby in her arms. She looked especially beautiful holding the infant.

"Thank you, everyone," Phoebe said. "I'm actually looking forward to the ambulance ride so I can get a little sleep."

Jo swished to Phoebe's bedside and brushed a palm

over her forehead. "Zach? Ben? Are you guys ready to go?"

"I've got the gurney right here," Ben called from the hallway.

Zach helped Ben move the gurney into the bedroom and carefully transferred Phoebe and Aaron onto it, pulling up the side rails so the two of them would be safe.

As he backed the rolling bed out of the room so they could maneuver it out of the house, his gaze landed once more on Delia. She was looking out the window. A single tear, glistening in the moonlight, rolled down her cheek. She swiped at it quickly and turned to make sure no one had been watching her.

He pretended to have his full attention on Phoebe and the baby, but he *had* seen.

Delia hadn't been crying happy tears.

She had been in agony.

Chapter Twenty-Two

Delia was mortified. She'd gritted her teeth until it hurt, and had clenched her fists until her nails had bit into her flesh, but despite her best efforts, a few tears had escaped from behind her eyes. She'd hurriedly dashed them away with her palms before they could wash down her face and hoped no one had seen.

It was bad enough that she felt this way on what should be the happiest of occasions, but it would be far worse for anyone to witness her momentary breakdown.

Fortunately, in all the excitement, no one had seemed to notice—least of all Zach, who, along with Ben, was busy preparing to transport Phoebe and baby Aaron to the hospital in San Antonio.

Now, as she drove back toward town, she wasn't so sure she could keep up pretenses any longer. She'd hoped to hold her feelings in check until after she'd returned home, but her raw emotions were pressing through even so.

The last thing she wanted to do was to give her son any reason to worry. He was already upset. He'd been sulking for days, presumably because she and Zach hadn't rushed to be together as a family after the new year had started.

She'd waited for Riley to raise the topic, just in case she was imagining problems where there were none; but so far, he hadn't said anything. She supposed his moping around the house and playing video games all day was telling enough. She was going to have to speak to him about it. Maybe in the morning, over a bowl of cereal.

She'd pulled herself together enough to gather her supplies and help Jo and Lucy clean up the bedroom before she left.

She'd never imagined anything could be as difficult as delivering this baby had been tonight—and it wasn't the complications with the baby's shoulder that had been so agonizing, either.

The way she and Zach had worked together to bring Aaron into this world safely was hands-down the most memorable moment of her life, with the exception of the night Riley was born. It trumped even the day she'd left Serendipity—and Zach—behind, in the sum of emotion she was now experiencing.

At least back then she'd thought she was doing the right thing. Now she knew without a doubt that practically every single decision she'd made since that moment had been wrong. She'd once imagined herself to have been unfairly drawn into a deep pit that she'd had to scrape and crawl her way to the top of on her own. But it occurred to her that in reality she'd been spiraling downward all this time.

And now?

Now she had hit rock bottom. She'd failed herself.

She'd failed Zach. She'd failed Riley. And most of all, she'd failed God.

Why hadn't she asked for the wise counsel of other, more mature Christians before she'd made such abrupt changes to her life and moved across the country? Why hadn't she taken the time to find a good church when she'd first arrived in Baltimore?

Why hadn't she sought out God's guidance every step of the way?

On her own, she'd managed to make a royal mess of everything. If she'd trusted God more, and had not been so hasty to have given up on Zach, maybe things would have been different. Maybe they would be a real family now, sharing a house together, and adopting a dog or two. Perhaps they would even have had more children by now, little brothers and sisters for Riley to play with and love.

But no.

She'd walked out on Zach when he'd needed her the most. She'd kept Riley's existence a secret from him, and had likewise kept Riley from knowing his dad. She'd ignored the still, small voice of God and followed a path of her own making.

And look where it had led her.

To a dark alley, alone, in the middle of the night.

Okay, so she was exaggerating just a little bit. She'd actually pulled in behind Cup o' Jo so she could toss the used linens in the trash. Even in the dark, Delia felt safe. This was Serendipity—her home.

But she did feel very much alone.

She popped the trunk of her car and scooped up the pile of delivery sheets, which were all rolled together in a lump. Using her shoulder to hold open the lid of the

Dumpster, she attempted to maneuver the large bundle into the trash, but the metal lid was too heavy for her and she had to drop the sheets at her feet.

She tried to flip back the top of the Dumpster with both hands, but something inside was catching and causing it to come crashing back down again.

With a frustrated cry, she tried one more time. Again, the lid slammed closed on her, this time scraping her elbow.

It wasn't a mortal wound. It was hardly a scratch, more annoying than painful. But it was the last straw for Delia. Like a precious vase being violently smashed to the ground, all the emotions she'd barely been keeping at bay exploded into a million razor-sharp shards in her chest.

Stifling a sob, she slid down the side of the Dumpster until her knees met the cold ground. She curled forward and pressed her palms to her eyes, rocking backward and forward as grief ruptured within her. She cried for all that could have been, and for all she should have done.

"Forgive me, Lord," she whispered raggedly. "I've ruined everything good You have given me."

She was so lost in her sorrow that she didn't hear the footsteps approaching her.

"Delia?" Zach's soft drawl gradually penetrated the thick, dark haze of emotion covering her. He crouched beside her and put a warm, comforting hand on her shoulder. "Princess? What is it? What's wrong?"

Zach?

What was he doing here? How had he found her?

"I followed you from the Hawkinses' house," he explained, even though she hadn't asked the question out loud. "I drove up just as you were leaving. I guess you didn't see me."

"But—" She caught herself on a sob. "Shouldn't you be driving Phoebe to San Antonio?"

A soft smile lit on his lips as he shook his head. "I had Ben drop me off at the station to switch out with another paramedic so I could come back and find you."

Delia drew in a sharp, ragged breath.

"It was time for the shift change anyway," he said, as if his appearance here was no more than a coincidence.

"Why?" She wanted to ask more, but all of her questions turned into jumbled phrases swirling around in her head.

"Why was there a shift change, or why did I come after you?" he teased.

She shook her head and then nodded.

"No to number one, yes to number two," Zach repeated aloud. "Got it."

She knew he was trying to make her smile, to loosen up a bit, but she just couldn't. Now that she'd let her guard down, there was nothing left for her except to scramble for her dignity.

She sat up a little straighter and looked him in the eye.

He brushed the back of his knuckles along the line of her chin, which only served to make her quiver even more than she already was, only this time it wasn't from the cold. "I knew something was bothering you. I wanted to find out what it was."

"H-how?"

She was stammering like an idiot, unable to complete more than one-word questions.

Zach didn't seem to notice. "I saw you crying back at the house."

She wanted to deny the meaning of her tears, but this was Zach. He knew her better than anyone, just as she knew him. He would not let this go until she told him what he wanted to hear.

The truth.

"I'm so sorry. I ruined everything," she explained, halting as she continued to sob.

"How is that?" he queried in a soft drawl.

"I ran away when I should have stayed and fought for you. I should have come home when I knew I was pregnant with Riley. You should have known your son, and he should have known his father."

Zach blew out a breath, then turned and slid to the ground with his back leaning against the Dumpster. Reaching for her shoulders, he gently pulled her into his arms.

"That's a lot of *should have's.*"

She hung her head. "I'm so ashamed of myself."

"You don't hold a candle to me." With a groan, he tightened his hold on her shoulder and brushed his mouth over her hair. "I've done things I don't even want to think about. I've shamed myself, you and most of all, God."

"But you've become such a fine Christian man," Delia protested. "You've done so many good things and helped so many people."

"And you haven't?" The tenor of his voice inched upward. "Don't you see, princess? This isn't a contest. God's not keeping score on what we've done right versus what we've done wrong. We'd never win that race. No one would."

"For by grace you have been saved, through faith, and this is not of yourselves, but it is the gift of God, so no one can boast." Delia didn't know where the scripture had come from. She hadn't studied the Bible in years. But somehow that old Sunday school verse had surfaced in her mind.

"I couldn't have said it better myself," he quipped.

"No, you couldn't," she agreed, leaning back so she could see into his eyes.

They sat quietly for a moment, each with their own thoughts, before Delia turned fully around in his arms.

"I still want you to know that I am deeply, profoundly sorry for all of my actions toward you, especially where Riley is concerned. I will do everything in my power to make up for the time I took away from you."

He tilted his head and flashed her the bad boy grin that once again stole her heart. "Yeah?"

"Yes," she repeated. "I don't know if you've thought about it yet, but I'm ready to comply with whatever custody arrangements you'd like."

"Oh, I've thought about it, princess," he said, his voice dropping to a low drawl.

She held her breath, waiting for him to drop the bomb, half expecting that he'd want more than fifty percent of the time with his son. Time that he deserved, and that she would willingly give, even if she was leaving a little bit of herself every time Riley walked out the door to go be with Zach.

"*Any* custody arrangement?" he clarified.

She broke her gaze away from him and nodded.

"Then I choose a hundred-percent custody. I want Riley to come and live with me full-time."

"What?" Her gaze returned to his with ferocity and she stood to her feet, burning with indignation. "But that's not fair. I mean, I want you to be in his life, but I can't just give him away to you."

He quirked his lips, but he didn't stand to meet her. "I never asked you to."

She shook her head. "I don't understand."

"It's fairly simple," he said, rolling to a crouch. "I want you and Riley both to move in with me—on a permanent basis."

"But—" she protested. Her heart was pounding any coherent thought out of her head.

"You can't go on living at your parents' house forever, and I have plenty of room."

"Yes, but—" She was strangling herself trying to speak.

"You've seen the place. It could use a woman's touch." His bad boy grin widened.

"I—" She didn't know what else to say.

"*Your* touch, Delia," he amended, leaning forward to take her hand in his. "I'm asking you to marry me."

"After all I've done to you? I thought you hated me."

He stood and reached for her other hand. "And I thought you wanted a platonic relationship. But both of us were mistaken." He paused. "Weren't we?"

He didn't sound quite so certain of himself anymore, and Delia couldn't keep him in limbo, not even for a second.

"I love you so much," she said, wrapping her arms around his neck and feathering kisses on his scratchy cheek. "I've always loved you."

He chuckled in relief and framed her face with his

hands. "There was never any woman but you, princess. Not ever."

If his words were not enough to convince her, his kiss certainly was. He poured every ounce of his love, and longing and passion into his kiss. He'd never been a man who'd gone halfway on anything, and now was no exception.

His lips were seeking an answer, and Delia gave it, returning his unspoken vow with her own. They were bound to each other by a spiritual thread as well as an emotional and physical one, and they always had been. God had granted her wish. And his wish.

And Riley's.

There was one more thing they needed to do.

"I love you, princess," he said, stroking her hair. "I hope we'll have our whole lives to keep telling each other and showing each other just how much."

She smiled softly and reached for his hand, lacing her fingers with his, feeling the strength of his grip and knowing he would always be there to love and protect his family.

"I think," she suggested, rubbing her thumb against his, "that we need to go wake up a certain anxious little boy and let him know his parents are getting married."

Zach leaned his forehead against hers, eye to eye.

"Yes we should," he agreed. "But because he's probably sleeping anyway, I think he can wait for a few more minutes." He lowered his head with a playful growl. "Daddy wants to kiss Mama again."

Epilogue

One Year Later

Riley Bowden-Ivers: Hey, Justin, this is so cool. I'm texting you a picture of an ultrasound my mom had.

Justin Sanderson: What is that? It looks like a bean.

Riley Bowden-Ivers: It's not a bean. It's my baby brother.

* * * * *

Dear Reader,

Welcome back to Serendipity, Texas, for the second book in the Email-Order Brides series. Many of the same characters who first appeared in *Phoebe's Groom* are back for more laughter, learning and love as childhood sweethearts Zach and Delia attempt to mend their relationship and move on as a family with their nine-year-old son, Riley. I hope you enjoy your return to Serendipity and the quirky characters I've grown to love while writing this series.

Next up in the Email-Order Brides series is *The Nanny's Twin Blessings*. This is the story of Drew Spencer and his adorable three-year-old twins. And if you've been following the romance between Cup o' Jo café owner Jo Murphy and cantankerous old Frank Spencer, be sure to catch this book—you won't be disappointed!

I love to hear from readers! Email me at DEBWRTR@aol.com, or look me up on Facebook.

Keep the faith,

Deb Kastner

Questions for Discussion

1. Delia knew she would run into Zach when she moved back to Serendipity. Why do you think she was so surprised when he showed up at the clinic with a patient?

2. Why didn't Delia inform Zach he was going to be a father when she first found out about the pregnancy? Do you think she was right or wrong to hold out on him? Why?

3. Was Zach ready to be a parent when Riley was conceived? What do you think would have happened if Delia had returned to Serendipity at that point?

4. Why do you think Delia chose a public place to introduce Riley to Zach? Was that the right decision? What would you have done?

5. How do you think Zach felt when he found out he had a son?

6. Delia's friends were stunned to find out a close friend had kept a major secret from them. Have you ever hid something, either physical or emotional, from your friends? Why?

7. What major themes run throughout this book? Which one is most important to you? Why?

8. Zach took a big chance not telling Delia about his plans for New Year's Eve. How would you have reacted in Delia's place? Have you ever had a surprise thrown at you?

9. Do you think Zach could truly be reformed? How was his heart changed throughout the course of the novel?

10. Delia's faith went by the wayside when she was in Baltimore. Do you think she could really lose her faith? Why or why not?

11. Which character did you most relate to in the novel? Why?

12. Riley was born into an age of divorce and single parenting and did not know his father until he was nine. Why do you think it was suddenly so important to him to have his mom and dad be together?

13. Sometimes both Zach and Delia wanted the same thing but managed to miscommunicate their feelings for each other. Describe a situation where you've encountered miscommunication between yourself and another. How did it happen, and how did you fix the problem?

14. Do you have your own children, or have you ever seen a baby being born (on television or in person)?

Is life a miracle of God, or is it simply science? Explain your answer.

15. What is the takeaway value of this book? What will you remember the most?

INSPIRATIONAL

Wholesome romances that touch the heart and soul.

COMING NEXT MONTH
AVAILABLE JANUARY 31, 2012

HOMETOWN HEARTS
The Granger Family Ranch
Jillian Hart

THE LAST BRIDGE HOME
Redemption River
Linda Goodnight

SECOND CHANCE MATCH
Chatam House
Arlene James

ROCKY POINT PROMISE
Barbara McMahon

FALLING FOR THE FIREMAN
Allie Pleiter

A HOUSE FULL OF HOPE
Missy Tippens